THIS MORTAL FLESH

To Josh and Jenny Lou

This Mortal Flesh

Bon Appetit!

A Novel of the Awakening Dead

Tony Simmons

ISBN: 1507738307
ISBN-13: 978-1507738306

DEDICATION

For Debra, Nathan, and Jessica.
With thanks to the Cheshires:
Mark, Carole, Marty, Rich, Ruth and Milinda

Other Fiction by the Author:

Tales of the Awakening Dead
The Book of Gabriel: An Endtimes Fable
Dragon Rising: Book One of The Shadow War
Welcome to the Dawning of a New Century
33 Days: Stories Inspired by the Songs of The Offer
The Best of Days: Short Stories and Miscellany

Visit TonySimmons.info for updates.

CHAPTER ONE: RESURRECTION DAY

I awoke in a state of ecstasy and terror, trembling, the soft flesh of a woman's forearm clamped between my numb fingers and shredding between my teeth. I yanked at the arm as a greater force pulled it away, but knowing the woman was dead, deader than me and not able to pull away, I glanced around and into the white eyes of a dead man staring at me.

He crouched on the sidewalk on the far side of the woman from me. Gnarled hands gripped her around her torso, and his face was buried in her throat. He growled and grunted, bit down harder and chewed. Dark blood, still fresh and warm, flowed around his jaws and across the woman's police uniform shirt.

Police … woman, I thought.

I let go, sat back roughly on the street, slowly becoming more aware of my surroundings. Pale hands, stained almost black with dried blood, rose in front of my face. My hands. Other people's blood.

I would have cried out, had there been air in my lungs.

I looked around, confused. Something had changed.

The sun was high and the sky clear, except for tendrils of smoke climbing into the calm blue. As far as I could see in either direction, similar scenes played out: Dead people sprawled in the street, truly dead, being eaten raw and fresh by pairs and groups of other dead people. A sea of monsters. Small fires burned in the remains of tall buildings and wrecked cars, the aftermath of larger fires that must have raged like the plague and then faded. Trash and bits of people's lives lay scattered on pavement.

It was very quiet. The background noise of life, extinguished, left only a distant crackling of flame, the soft moans of the diners as they forced air into and out of useless lungs. And oh, I knew the reason they moaned, the overwhelming desire beyond all thought. I knew, as well, that they did not really think at all — just needed, violently required, madly craved. I could feel it welling up in my brain like a hot knife, or rather, like a pain that might only be quenched by a hot knife.

The hunger.

I felt sluggish, a child waking from a long sleep, bad dreams not yet forgotten in the fog of awakening. I was dead, I knew. Or rather, undead. A zombie, in the jargon of the times. If I were alive, I'd have laughed at the idea. Or I'd have run screaming, and then I'd have been overwhelmed by the biters and clawers, the groaners and chewers, eaten raw and fresh.

But I was not alive, and I neither laughed nor screamed. I sat and thought about that, recognizing even as I did so that the act of thinking was, itself, something of a miracle in my condition. I tried to remember what I had been, how this had begun, what I had learned about the zombies before — what happened to me?

In the moment, however, I couldn't muster enough enthusiasm to maintain curiosity. To care. I would either recall or not recall. It didn't matter. Right now, more importantly, fresh meat lay only an arm's reach away, and I had to have it.

I grabbed the dead woman's ankle and lifted her leg to my mouth, and as I bit into the muscular backside of her calf, the other zombie who was eating her snatched at the body again, jerking her loose from my grip. He didn't look at me. I didn't matter to him. He had no concept of a threat to his person or desires. His thought process, such as it was, stopped at the realization that I was a zombie too, and thus, not food. The yanking was as instinctual to him as the hunger, and I wouldn't have noticed him either a few minutes ago, merely yanked back until I got the bite for which I was searching. We'd have pulled the woman apart between us.

This wouldn't do.

I stared down the street again, seeing all the walking dead — none of which seemed to be thinking beyond the search for fresh flesh. No living humans about. No one ran for their lives. No live food, but lots of hungry corpses on the move. They shuffled and stumbled. Some of them crawled. Some sat like rag dolls and moaned, waiting for a victim to come close.

No, I thought again, this simply must stop. Too many feeders, not enough to eat. Someone ought to do something.

I shifted my focus, looking closer around me, now, for whatever weapons might be at hand. Trash littered the street, debris from burning buildings and wrecked vehicles, items dropped in some panicked mob's mad and futile dash for escape. Canned food, water bottles. Single shoes.

On a sidewalk across the street, a broken Louisville Slugger lay in a small puddle of viscous drippings. A little further along was a shotgun.

I got to my feet, swayed as I discovered that my muscles worked differently than I was used to. Numb feet made balance and forward motion a challenge. I took an interminable time to stumble over to the shotgun. Tried to pick it up. Nearly lost my balance. Stumbled backward.

On my second try, the gun slipped from my stiff fingers. I stood over it, looking at it, trying to remember what it was. Double barrel, what my grandfather called an "aught-six." No, that was wrong, I thought. A 12-gauge. Yes.

I straightened, looked around. A couple of the — I had no other word — a couple of the *zombies* eating down the road had noticed my movement and eyed me. They found me lacking as food, and turned away.

I reached for the gun again, carefully wrapping my fingers on the stock and barrel, and clutching it. I could almost feel it, as if my hands had gone to sleep, but no stinging sensation followed; my limbs, like my brain, seemed slow to wake up. I brought the gun up to my chest, pressed the catch, and opened the breach. One bright red shell remained intact. I looked around to see if other shells had been dropped nearby, but didn't spot any.

One shot.

I crossed back to my hungry breakfast companion and the dead police woman, and wondered if the gun had belonged to her. Where was her sidearm? Probably tossed down somewhere. More importantly, I discovered movement was becoming easier, perhaps because I was making a conscious effort. I placed the business end of the barrel against the dead man's head, braced myself for the kick, and pulled the trigger.

I fell over, completely unable to maintain my stance, as a blast like thunder rebounded and echoed up and down the street. I rose up on my elbows to see what remained of the other man.

Everything but his head, it turned out.

Then I heard the approaching moans. The gun blast had drawn their attention. All along the street, the dead turned away from their meals and headed in my direction, expecting to find something warmer and more to their taste. They exited buildings, crawled from wrecks, lurched around corners. Dozens of them, perhaps tens of dozens.

I should have known better. My memory of a sense of self-preservation attempted to trigger a fight-or-flight response; I was vaguely aware that I should be terrified. I was not terrified. Not even concerned. I felt little more than a detached curiosity as the individuals gathered into groups, then the crowd grew closer from both directions.

What could they do, really? Kill me?

I got to my feet again, stood still and waited for them, holding the spent gun in my left hand. A couple of them lost interest at a distance and veered off, looking for food once more. The first to draw close hit his knees, the bastard, and started chewing on the same forearm I had been eating when I awoke.

Three of them got right up in my space, sniffed me. One with jowls like an English bulldog made ready to lick me, then noticed the dead woman at my feet and joined the buffet line.

I waited for the rest of them to disperse. They wandered aimlessly, apparently as disinterested in the police woman as they were in me.

I raised the gun over my head and used the stock like a club, whacking both of the eaters in their brainpans. The beefy one went down with a sigh of escaping methane. Then I sat down to finish my meal in peace and think about this further, but as I bit into the woman's soft flesh, I stopped thinking at all.

This. This was everything. It was why I existed.

This mortal flesh.

**

CHAPTER TWO: THE LAND OF TERROR

Jane backed away from the Z, her feet scattering trash across the tile floor. The dead woman had been hidden in the laundry room closet, lurking there since her death, and fell over when Jane opened the door. She had not surprised Jane, though, because Jane knew how to open doors; after the world ends, you stand aside just in case of lurkers, and you have your weapon ready and your exits in sight.

Jane didn't need an exit this time. The dead woman went down hard on her hands and knees as she fell out of the pantry, and Jane only stepped back far enough to keep her balance and swing her hatchet.

She called her hatchet "George." George was very sharp, and when not in use, it dangled on a strap from Jane's forearm. George cleaved the back of the dead woman's skull, spattering black brain and the ink these things used for blood across the apartment's nice ceramic tile.

Jane drew George back immediately and listened for

movement or moans elsewhere in the apartment.

She licked dry lips.

Satisfied by the quiet, Jane stepped over the corpse to check the pantry for supplies, hoping to find some food. She picked up a half-gallon jug of bleach and put it in her knapsack; pouring bleach in your path had been shown to confuse a pack of Zs long enough to aid an escape. It screwed with their freakish sense of smell. She ignored the other cleaning supplies and the scented dryer sheets. There was no food in here.

Jane closed the laundry room door, marked an X on it with a piece of sidewalk chalk. She grabbed the sack of cans and boxed food she'd found in the kitchen, closed the outer door and marked it with an X as well.

At this rate, she figured, she could clear this floor of apartments and be back to home base before dark. She added the new sack to a small pile of canned food, sealed boxes, and bags of dry edibles she had already gathered by the fire escape at the end of the corridor; she would bring some people back in the morning with her to get the stash.

This was what she did.

Jane was not her name, just what everyone called her. She didn't care. They called her Jane because one of the men had joked she was fast as a cheetah, slippery as a python, and strong as an elephant. She also had been known to swing from building to building on ropes and cables, dangling above the Zs like Tarzan on a vine over a pool of snapping crocodiles. The modern equivalent of a jungle girl.

The man who first called her "Jane" was dead now. His name was Paul. He had been bitten, and she had busted his head with a lead pipe rather than see him turn.

She preferred her hatchet to a lead pipe. She had named her hatchet after another famous jungle lord, the one who tended to smack into trees when he swung around on vines. She hadn't told anyone that story. No one had asked.

Jane turned 21 on her last birthday, which happened two weeks to the day before the first plague reports hit the news. She was pretty sure that had been a couple of months ago, though time had gotten itself mixed up after the world died. It was difficult to be certain.

The sea of time ebbed, now a stagnant pool. The weather should have begun turning by now, growing colder with the autumn, but the days remained as hot as July and she could smell the asphalt melting when the breeze stilled. Some people claimed the earth spun more slowly since it had died, that days and nights stretched longer than they had been before the plague. Jane didn't know about that, nor did it really matter to her, so long as the world kept turning.

So long as day followed night, then Jane believed that death eventually followed even those who refused to lie down. Whenever possible, Jane liked to be the one who helped death along.

At the moment, she stalked the top floor of a ten-story building off Market Avenue; the top seven floors were apartments, and the lower ones offices, and she knew she would find most of the food up high, where the elevation and the afternoon sun gave her a clear view of Zs wandering a few blocks away, near an older structure that raged with flame; they seemed drawn to the spectacle, the movement of the light and smoke. Or perhaps, the aroma of people cooking inside.

It amazed her that this sort of random destruction still happened. During the plague, fires started because of wrecks, or plane crashes, or stupid people setting fire to Zs, not realizing they would just keep walking around like mobile matchsticks, spreading flames everywhere they went until they were too damaged to keep moving. Fires happened back then because someone left a stove burning, or an electric iron plugged in. Later, fires erupted because of electrical shorts in damaged or untended houses, but soon enough there was no more electricity.

These days, the fires tended to begin with big booms caused by gas leaks. She wondered what had set this one off — then she realized it wasn't a big deal. She didn't care. It didn't matter, so long as it didn't spread toward the junkyard her group called their Compound. There was a job to be done, and no sense wondering about things that didn't put food on the table.

Her father had said much the same thing to her when she told him a year ago that she was switching her college major to physics. He wanted her to earn a business degree. She preferred to talk to people smarter than her about the origins of the universe.

Now all she wanted was to locate some Hershey bars that hadn't melted.

That was her mission in life. Who she was, what she did. Not Hershey bars, exactly, but finding food. Jane was good at scavenging, had a knack for uncovering intact caches, but the search for unspoiled food had become more difficult as the weeks wore on, and she had to probe farther afield every opportunity. Searching buildings close to the Compound had been easier; they were smaller than these downtown, and they had served as training grounds, letting her hone Z-killing skills and build confidence while helping to feed the other survivors.

They had walled themselves into a junkyard at the end of a dead-end street near the docks. Over time, they systematically cleared each building on the block, boarding up ground-floor windows and doors, and erecting barriers of junk between the buildings to dissuade any Zs from entering their safe zone. Zs don't climb, as such — though when they moved in great numbers, as at the height of the plague, they sometimes piled up, one upon the next, and crawled across each other like swarms of insects traversing flooded gullies.

Jane taught the others what she learned — how to clear a building, first climbing to the roof by fire escape and working her way down, floor by floor, room by room.

She checked each closet, every pantry, any cabinet large enough for even a small child to hide inside, and that's how she found more than a few Zs like this last woman. Too often, people hid themselves after being attacked, died in the closed cabinet or closet, turned, and revived trapped and hungry, too stupid to twist a doorknob.

Although Maxwell, their leader, frowned upon anyone going into zombie territory alone, Jane considered herself an exception to his rules. On her own today, scouting ahead of the scavenger squad for likely food stores, she hoped to chance upon a cache hoarded by less-lucky survivors. She didn't fear bad karma for wishing for such a thing, as there had been lots of less-lucky survivors, a lot more than the few fortunate ones with whom she now lived; their food had to be hidden somewhere. She'd found no big score, but lots of small ones would keep the Compound alive a little while longer.

Jane turned away from the window and eased back into the corridor that ran the length of the floor. Eight apartments on each floor. Two bedrooms each. Sixteen closets. Eight bathrooms with cabinets and closets. Eight kitchens with cabinets and pantries. Eight laundry rooms, eight coat closets, numerous beds under which the dead could lurk.

She hated looking under beds. Fucking hated it.

Jane already had cleared three apartments on this floor, marking them and closing or jamming shut the doors. She double checked that her escape route remained clear and the door to the stairwell was wedged shut, and she headed to the next apartment.

Listened at the door, tried the handle. Locked. Rattled the handle.

A sound. Something thumped inside, like a book falling off a table, or a chair overturning. Jane knocked on the door.

A creature inside the apartment moaned, struck the door, and Jane glimpsed its shadow moving in the dim light peeking underneath the door. She waited, listening for signs of other creatures joining it to push and scratch and pound on the door; if she heard more than one, she would skip this apartment until she returned with the rest of her crew tomorrow; she'd mark the door with a big O, and inside the O she would write a number estimating how many Zs were inside.

After a few minutes of listening, Jane decided the moaner was alone. One Z she could deal with. She breathed slowly, still listening to it, as she worked up her nerve.

It sounded sad. Not angry, not even desperate. It sounded lonely.

Jane wanted to put it out of its misery.

She swung her right arm out, and George slapped into her palm at the end of its strap. Jane kicked the door twice before it slammed open, knocking the lonely Z off its feet. It had been a young man when it lived; it wore a T-shirt from her college.

Jane scanned the room quickly, saw no other opponents, strode into the apartment and introduced the Z to George.

Only later did she wonder what his major was.

**

CHAPTER THREE: MAD EYES

The world plunged into darkness, all at once. Or so it seemed.

I had walked for hours, spotting no living person and few moving dead ones once I left downtown. And I paused only once for a cold snack — part of a man tangled in the wreckage of a motorcycle. I broke off a forearm at the compound fracture where the bone jutted through the ruptured skin, and carried it with me, gnawing when the hunger hit. I found the meat unappetizing, but it kept me moving.

I considered the prospect of a survivor shooting me as I walked, but it felt less and less probable the farther I proceeded. The suburbs were empty. Most people had panicked when the news broke, and had jumped into their cars, making for the interstates and the inevitable traffic snarls. Those who stayed behind, like my family and me, were dead now, or mostly so. No one lingered in the homes but ghosts and things that should have been ghosts.

The buildings grew smaller to either side of my route, and farther apart, until greenbelts gave way to trees and narrow streets lined with modern houses. I saw no lights in any of the houses, neither electric nor candle flame. Several along the way were boarded up, and I allowed for the possibility live people still hunkered within these, though I didn't catch their scent. Most stood open, the large picture windows smashed, doors cracked and creaking in the evening breeze.

I became aware of the darkness when I found myself standing outside the house I remembered as the place where we had lived, my girls and I. My wife and daughter. My family.

Home.

A two-story wood frame structure with stone work facing the street. A wooden privacy fence surrounded the back yard. Like others along the way, the front door stood open. The interior, black as my blood, darker than the night sky.

My night vision seemed unnaturally vibrant. I clearly saw the upper torso of a human body rotting in the front yard. It didn't have the ravaged appearance of one that had been ripped apart by zombies, but rather looked to have been dragged here and stripped by an animal.

I had heard dogs barking in the distance during my trek, and now I wondered what damage packs of them might do to a lone wandering dead man.

I threw down the last of the arm I had been snacking on and strode inside the house. Seeing the place further awakened my brain. I began to recall more of my former existence as the triggers hit me — photos on the mantle, a pile of empty food cans and boxes drawing flies in the kitchen sink, tools piled by the back door that I had used to try to seal the place.

The six-foot fence in the back yard was sturdy and had kept the trouble out, but the bay windows up front had been our undoing. The memory rose fresh in my vision of undead pouring through the shattered window, clambering over one another like rats once they had our spoor.

I stumbled down the hall to the master bedroom, shuffling through trash and rotten debris in the gloom. Pieces of the smashed bedroom door lay scattered in the hallway, but I didn't remember the dead doing that. It looked like it had been broken down from inside the bedroom. Who had done that? Me?

I concentrated. I recalled rushing my wife and daughter — my two girls, I called them — into the room just ahead of the mob as they crowded each other to follow us in the hall. I held the door against their onslaught while Julia hammered boards across it into the studs and Ella — *Ellie? Eleanor?* — Eleanor ran into the bathroom.

But something wasn't right. I recalled feeling dizzy. Weak. "I feel fine," I assured them.

Soon, we crouched together in the darkness beside the bathtub, which we had filled with water before the pipes lost pressure. We listened to the creatures pounding on the bedroom door, moaning and hissing. They never tired, but we did. No matter how terrified, we were only human. We fell asleep finally, overcome by fear and exhaustion.

I remembered a dream, or maybe a hallucination. Something about a creek I used to swim in when I was a kid. A face under the water. "I've just seen a face," I recalled saying.

But that was it. Nothing else. I didn't remember anything more until my awakening today in the city. I must have died in that bathroom with Julia and Eleanor, and I must have killed them when I returned from the dead. I wondered if I would find them wandering around inside.

Now I walked through the bedroom and into the bathroom, finding my way more by muscle memory than sight. I slid aside the privacy door to the little space housing the toilet and tub, and I saw them in there. What was left of them.

My girls.

I didn't remember eating them, but it's the only thing that made sense, considering the condition of their remains. I must have killed them and eaten them, rendering them unable to reanimate. Only stringy bits clung to their bones, and curdled skin to broken skulls.

I didn't recall figuring out how to open the bathroom door or pounding on the bedroom door until it finally gave out. I didn't remember wandering into the streets or following the herd of hungry dead into the more densely populated city. I didn't even know how long I'd been dead.

And I didn't know what to do next. What was appropriate. What mattered.

I stood in that spot and stared at the bones, the rotted meat and tattered clothing of the two people on earth who were supposed to mean something to me, and I felt nothing. Nothing.

I waited for the sun to rise. I waited for the hunger to return and bring with it that wonderful ecstasy of forgetfulness.

Then I heard the dog growling in the room behind me.

I looked at it, and I thought about how to breathe, made my muscles pull, and gasped a ragged breath, managing to croak out something like "Rock."

The dog was mine. Ours. Family pet. A small Labrador mix. We called him "Rocky." Short haired and golden, though currently he was mostly black, his fur matted with mud and dried blood, his eyes wild.

He'd been in the living room with us when the horde crashed through the bay window. Must have run through the doggy door into the back yard when we ran for the bedroom. Must have come back through the house as the crowd thinned.

I looked back at the corpses in the bathroom and recalled the stripped body on the front lawn, and didn't have to ask myself what Rocky had been eating while I was gone.

He crouched and growled again, but his ears wiggled, meaning he was confused. His tail wagged and then stopped. He recognized me, but I smelled wrong. He didn't know whether to attack or nuzzle for petting.

I decided to ignore him and see what happened. I got the flashlight off the bathroom vanity, where I'd left it before I died, and pointed it into the big mirror, trying to get a clear look at myself. I needed to determine what kind of shape I was in before I headed back out into the world to hunt for food.

Curiosity. A basic survival mechanism. It may have killed the cat, but it also led hominids to figure out how to hunt. The thought reminded me: I was an anthropologist in my previous life. A college professor, I believed. Doctor … something.

I couldn't remember my name. But recalling my vocation helped make sense of my clinical view of the situation. Studying this new social order would be only natural.

But first, I had to survive.

I took inventory of myself. I wore a leather jacket with a cotton hoodie, a black button-up shirt, jeans, and sneakers. I didn't remember putting on the hoodie or jacket; maybe Julia put them on me when my fever turned to chills.

My clothes were torn, but most of my skin appeared intact. Like the other undead I had seen today, my pale flesh was dry, mottled from bruising, and riddled with blackish veins visible through strangely translucent skin. I looked to be in worse shape than I really was because of the coagulated blood all over me. I stank of death, but some of that stink had come from the food I'd been eating and the crowd I'd run with, so to speak.

I shrugged out of the jacket and ripped open my shirt. Popping buttons was simply easier than using numb fingers to unbutton them. My torso appeared undamaged, though blackened on the left side, where blood must have pooled after I died. I was grateful, if that was the right word, for being a health nut in life: Muscle tone looked decent, abs solid. I would last a while like this, if the rot could be controlled.

Was I even rotting? I couldn't be certain. I hadn't drawn any flies, not like my two girls had done.

Rocky settled on the floor, scratched my discarded shirt, and sniffed it. He kept his distance.

I needed fresh clothes. But I also needed weapons — both to put down the zombies and to protect myself from humans. And considering that prospect gave me an idea about a protective suit that might help me hold things together and conceal my condition from a distant observer. Something that might help me get close enough to food without tipping it off that I was hunting.

My next-door neighbor had been a scuba instructor. An adjunct at the college where I taught. He took me on several diving excursions over the years. A little taller than me and heavier, but I figured I could make one of his diving suits work. He also had headgear and masks, and some of those little harpoon shooters used for spear fishing.

The more I thought about it, the more I became convinced the idea was solid.

Shining the flashlight ahead of me, I walked back through my house and onto the lawn. A dead man standing in the street turned my way, his attention drawn by the moving light. We stared at each other for several seconds. I shined the light at him.

He lacked a left hand and the left side of his face. His lips had peeled off, and I saw crooked teeth sparkling in the beam. He must have been confused as hell, seeing a light being carried by something that wasn't food.

After a few more seconds, he turned away, continued toward wherever he had been headed, and I crossed the lawn to the next house over. The front door was closed, the windows boarded shut. I lifted the little brass knocker on the door and tapped it several times.

The dead man in the street moaned and turned. I glanced back at him. He stumbled toward me.

I tapped the knocker again, shave-and-a-haircut rhythm.

Someone tapped back on the other side of the door. Two bits. I realized I could smell the person, the sweat and urine. I could tell there was a living human being on the other side of the door just by the stink of it.

It smelled delicious.

The dead man behind me groaned and tripped at the curb, but righted himself and came closer.

I tapped shave-and-a-haircut. Two bits answered.

I gasped, pulling in air, and huffed at the doorway, "Help! Help me!"

Locks clicked on the other side of the door and it eased open. The security chain flickered in the beam of my flashlight, and a tiny, frightened boy's voice said, "Are you bit?"

"Not yet. Please!"

The boy closed the door and unlatched the chain. The dead man got there just then and shoved against me. I let him pass and pushed him ahead of me into the house.

Gunshots echoed, loud in the night, but the zombie took both bullets. Then I shoved inside, clubbing the boy's arm with my flashlight. I saw his eyes, round and big in a skinny pale face. His pistol clattered across the floor. He screamed.

The house was pitch black except for the beam of the light swinging and swinging as I clubbed first the boy and then the zombie that was trying to rise off the floor. The lens smashed, and the light winked out, but I kept striking them, first one and then the other.

The screaming stopped. Both of them moaned, but after a couple more blows, the moaning stopped too.

Finally, neither of them moved. I licked the boy's blood off of the broken flashlight and experienced a sensation like fireworks exploding inside my skull. He lay unconscious on the floor beside the dead man, close to death himself.

I tried to dredge up the boy's name. Gary? Greg? Eleanor had caught the school bus with him since we had moved here two years ago. *Gideon.* That was it. Sixth grade. Played soccer. Fellowship of Christian Athletes.

I looked around to see if any other people lurked in the house, but the silence had returned and I could find no stink of life but his. Gideon was alone. Somehow, he had survived here all by himself.

I picked up his gun and stuck it in the back of my pants. Went to close the door and saw Rocky hovering on the stoop.

"Come on … Rocky, boy," I said, and speaking came easier this time, taking two breaths to complete. With practice, I would be able to carry on a conversation.

Rocky entered the dark house and sniffed the zombie. He bit the creature's left stump and tore off some meat. His tail wagged.

I pulled Gideon up by the T-shirt and bit into his throat. The hot blood was like cool water to a man lost in a desert wasteland. It made my brain buzz, my skin tingle. I had a sensation in my chest as if my heart raced, but even then I recognized it as only a trick of firing neurons in my head, like the phantom pains after an amputation. An itch that could be scratched only through flesh and blood.

I would have to explore these feelings, try to figure out how they were produced. Why my brain wanted meat and blood so desperately. How my muscles remained flexible and mobile when I was, for all intents and purposes, no longer alive. I would need to understand these things if I wanted to survive.

And I did want to survive. It was my chief instinct: Keep moving and feed the hunger.

I gnawed off more of the boy's throat meat, hearing the muscles snap, smelling the coppery aroma of blood, and I wondered again how Gideon had survived on his own in this house. I chewed and swallowed. And as I chomped down on him again, I decided I didn't care how he had managed to stay alive, as long as the rest of him tasted this good.

**

CHAPTER FOUR: THE LOST OASIS

Jane stood in the open window of a third floor office overlooking the Compound, and balanced on the edge. She shifted her backpack, flexed her shoulders, and gripped the loops tied in the end of a dead electrical cable that dangled from a lamp post just inside the wall of junk that marked the Compound's perimeter. Weeks ago, she had rigged the cable in case she needed to get into the junkyard in a hurry. She thought it made sense to test it from time to time.

The usual entrance route was up a fire escape and through the top floor of the Ashmore Building on the camp's perimeter. The bolt-holes hidden in the junk wall were designed to open only from the inside. She wanted another way in, if she needed it.

She eyeballed her landing zone: a stack of old mattresses just past the junk wall. She took a deep breath, stepped out of the window, and swung in a lazy arc over the wrecked cars and scrap metal blocking the cross street. She released the cable just as her swing began to arc upward again, managing a heavy landing on both feet. The cans in her backpack clattered and shifted, but she kept her footing.

Jane looked up when she heard the slow clap coming from Maxwell. He stood watch from the roof of an old dump truck parked in the street. His big claw-head hammer hooked over an elbow, chrome shimmering in the starlight.

"I give you a nine for style," he said.

"The Russian judge only awards threes," she answered. "That leaves it in the hands of the French."

"You never know," he said.

Jane shrugged out of the backpack and unzipped it as she walked over to the truck. She'd brought along several cans of beans, corn, and Thick'n'Hearty soup that she'd liberated from the Market Avenue building. She'd have carried more, except she had to leave room for the bleach bottle, which she ditched after splashing her trail two blocks away, just in case something followed her.

Jane tossed Maxwell a can of the pot roast and potatoes soup. He caught it one-handed and glanced at it, angling it to allow the ambient starlight to play on its bright surface. His hand dwarfed the can.

"Tonight we feast," he said and tossed it back down to her.

The cans would go into the shared cache, and everyone would get an equal portion. Soups generally got stretched with water anyway. Maxwell would wait until his shift ended before grabbing some food. That was just one of the understandings here.

"Are you okay?" he asked.

She sighed. "I'm so tired."

Jane climbed up the side of the dump truck and joined him on the roof. The perch was high enough to serve as an observation post, and the truck could still be driven if the need arose. From here, a lookout could see the length of the dark avenue and over the junk walls of two side streets. Another guard sat watch at the entrance to the actual junkyard at the other end of the street, and Jane gave a wave in that direction. She saw a brief movement of white cloth as the guard waved a signal flag in answer.

"It's been quiet today," Maxwell said, shifting the big hammer from one hand to the other and transferring the strap to the new wrist. "Not a single Z in the neighborhood."

She asked if any people had shown up, and he shook his head. They hadn't seen a live person in weeks. They figured any survivors were holed up, like them, and getting by the same way, scavenging canned food from apartments in the city. No one wandered alone any more.

No one but Jane.

"Plenty of Zs on Market Avenue," she said. "No people. I made it that far today, and started clearing an apartment building. Found a good stash of edibles. I'll take the crew out tomorrow."

Maxwell nodded. He was the de facto leader of their group, and she knew he didn't like her to recon alone. He was protective of all the Compound people, just as she was. It was a thing they shared. But she also had long ago made it clear that nothing could keep her from going if she really wanted to leave.

He towered over her, a lean but powerful figure. His naturally red skin seemed darker in the fading light, and his sharp features reminded her of a Native American she had seen on TV once, crying over the damage people were doing to the earth. Maxwell didn't strike her as the crying type.

"I got worried when you didn't make it back by dark," he said. He always said something when she returned from a jaunt into the jungle on her own, something to let her know that he cared.

Jane leaned into his shoulder for a playful nudge. They grinned at each other and didn't say anything more for a little while. She allowed the contact to linger in the silence. It was nice, comforting, almost like being with her father or grandfather. Maxwell was somewhere between their ages, in his fifties, and he was one of only two people in the Compound that Jane would touch at all — or who would let Jane touch him, for that matter. When you fear bites, wounds of any kind, the transfer of germs, then who would risk physical contact with a person who willingly exposes herself to Zs every day?

Jane shrugged and stretched her arms, cracked her knuckles.

Maxwell leaned away. She noticed that he had never stopped scanning the perimeter. His vigilance didn't make her feel more secure; it just reinforced how vulnerable they remained, even behind the walls of junk. If enough of the Zs gathered out there — well, she remembered the televised images of the sea of dead piling up against Army barricades, climbing over each other and over-running the last human encampments before the lights went out. The same thing could happen here at any moment of the day or night if a large enough mob found them.

"You better go get some rack time if you're taking the crew shopping tomorrow," Maxwell said.

She nodded and climbed down from their perch, picked up the backpack, and trudged to the Compound entrance. They didn't have any words or waves of parting. No one said goodbye anymore. It was another thing that was just understood.

The gate guard, Nancy, let Jane through the levered entry without a word. The metal fencing rose high enough for Jane to stoop under it, then fell back in place; Jane heard the clank as Nancy locked down the counterweights behind her.

The sound was too loud, Jane thought. It carried in the quiet of this dead hour. The wrong ears might hear.

Jane lugged her backpack to the kitchen, an aluminum-sided bungalow that had been the tiny living space for the old man who owned the junk yard before the end of the world. He was dead now, and twenty-seven strangers lived here. They slept in a school bus that they had converted into bed space using the back seats from old cars, mattresses scrounged from area buildings, and other bits of junk.

One by one, or in small groups, they had found their ways here in the days and weeks after the plague hit. The first few to arrive were dead now, too, victims of scavenging raids gone wrong, or illness, or suicide. But the population leveled off, and they organized enough to figure out how to run the forklifts and use the daylight hours to move around the junk and increase their safe zone. They learned to scavenge and survive, worked out schedules for keeping watch, cooking, even doing laundry in barrels of rain water captured with makeshift funnel systems built from car hoods and rubber engine tubing.

Her new tribe had few rules, chief of which was that anyone infected or bitten gets put down without hesitation. It worked for them, so far.

Jane hesitated at the door to the school bus. She looked at the faded number beside the door, 42, and wondered if it had any significance. She knew nothing about numerology, but as a lifelong science geek she had picked up a sci-fi reading habit and she knew the number was jokingly referred to as the answer to the question of "life, the universe and everything." She didn't expect she would live long enough to learn the question.

The bus' original folding Plexiglas door had been replaced by a sheet of metal bolted to an old oak table; it latched on the inside, but the latch could be thrown by turning a crank below the step. Jane unlatched the door and called out, "It's Jane," before mounting the steps into the darkness.

She heard Joey call back, "Hey Jane," and she knew it was safe to enter; no one would try clubbing her in the dark.

She latched the door behind her and mussed Joey's mop top as she passed the child in the aisle. He was the only other person here, besides Maxwell, she would touch. In fact, he was her touchstone; that moment of contact helped her to relax, reassured her brain that she was as safe as it was possible to be. Then she dropped, exhausted, into her bunk and went right to sleep.

She never remembered her dreams. She was grateful for that small blessing.

**

CHAPTER FIVE: THE MONKEY SUIT

I didn't sleep. I never tired. But I hungered.

Through that first night of reawakening, I searched first my neighbor's house for whatever tools I might need, and then my own for whatever might spark memory, and always I thought of food.

I didn't think I'd been dead for very long because I had not rotted like so many of the carcasses in the streets or even the ones in my bathroom. But Gideon had been keeping a calendar, and it looked like he'd been doing so for a few months. I kept going back to savor more of his tender flesh, and I wondered if we had worked together, his family and mine, to survive for a while; I had trouble focusing on that part of my memory, and it suggested parts of my brain were deader than others.

How many holes in my brain? A sea of holes?

I found Gideon's father's — what was his name? Bill? I think he was Bill — I found Bill's wetsuits and other dive gear in the garage. I stripped out of what remained of my gore-caked clothing and wiped down with a damp cloth I found in the bathroom. Getting into the suit wasn't easy, even though it was a size too large for me. My fingers were clumsy, but my muscle control increased the more I struggled. I wondered how much dexterity I might regain, considering the neuropathy that made everything feel numb.

I sat on the floor of the garage and wiggled my feet through the legs of the suit, then worked my hands through the tight arm holes. Getting the zipper strap positioned over my shoulder so I could yank up the back zipper was the most difficult and time-consuming part of the process.

I did not get frustrated. The dead don't get frustrated. We are as patient as the dirt.

We do, however, grow hungry. Several times during the night I lost track of what I was trying to accomplish as the craving fogged my thoughts. Once, I realized I had crawled into the living room to gnaw on the boy's cold meat, still trailing the wetsuit wrapped around my ankles. My knees and elbows suffered light abrasions, which was precisely what I had been attempting to avoid by putting on the wetsuit.

The constant hunger meant I had to figure out a way to keep fresh food close at hand. And a method to keep the food alive longer, even as I dined. It was a puzzle. I could solve it. I believed I had been pretty clever when I was alive.

Primitive cannibal tribes believed that one gained strength by eating the heart of one's enemy. They would consume the wise men of other tribes in order to steal their wisdom, or devour the corpses of fallen warriors to absorb their prowess. I wondered, if we truly are what we eat, then perhaps I could become stronger and smarter if I consumed a higher grade of food.

Finally secured in the suit, I went into Gideon's bathroom so I could inspect the fit. It bunched at the crotch and armpits, and it didn't quite seal at the wrists and ankles, but it would do the job. The suit would protect my skin from tears if I fell or had to fight off an attacker or reluctant food, and it would hide the appearance of my skin from a casual observer.

Now, I needed to find some decent gloves and shoes, and some head gear. Something to cover my dead face and something to shield my brain from puncture or bullet holes. Maybe some elbow and knee pads.

Bill had a pair of heavy leather boots he wore when he took his Harley out on weekends. I remembered Bill always prided himself on how "extreme" he was. Diving, biking, parachuting. I wondered where he was now, and if getting there had been extreme enough for him.

I put on a pair of Bill's socks, then slid on the scuba suit's booties, then put on Bill's boots; all the padding helped them fit me. I pulled the straps on the side of the boots tight and walked around in them, getting a feel for the weight and movement. They would work, but I wouldn't be doing any running. I was not a fast zombie.

I pulled the wetsuit head piece on and attached its Velcro seals at the neck. It covered my nose and mouth, leaving only my eyes exposed. This was looking better all the time. Some tinted safety glasses with an elastic band would complete the disguise, and I had those in my garage next door.

I tried Bill's scuba gloves, but they were too large and clumsy for me. I needed batting gloves or driving gloves. Lamb skin. Something I could wear and still use a pistol. Or a Taser?

What was I thinking of? Why was I thinking about a Taser? No, not one of those. A stun gun.

I went back to my house. Rocky followed, though he still kept his distance. He brought along somebody's bone to gnaw.

My wife had carried a stun gun in her purse, one of those crackling prods you could touch to someone and incapacitate them with 50,000 volts. She used to clutch it in her hand when she went to her car after a late shift at the hospital. She never had to use it, but I could; it would take the fight out of the food, if I could get close enough. It didn't fire leads at the target like a Taser; it had to be pressed against the body and activated.

But in order to carry it, I would need pockets, or a tool belt. A utility belt. I could get one from a hardware store, maybe, something with pouches and loops for hammers and such.

I found the purse on the floor of the bedroom closet. I spilled the contents on the bed and rooted through them. Tissues, makeup bag, bottle of generic headache pills — that sparked another idea I would pursue later — keys, cell phone, package of mints.

Stun gun.

The morning sun was a dim golden glow through the broken bedroom windows as I pushed the button on the grip of the gun. The head of it crackled, and I caught the blue-white light reflecting in the mirror of my wife's vanity table. I saw myself there, a tall man in a black body suit and boots, with dead, white eyes staring back at me.

"I'm … Batman," I said to the reflection.

**

CHAPTER SIX: THE MINDLESS MONSTERS

Joey brought Jane a cup of black coffee to wash down her Thick'n'Hearty breakfast soup. He was ten years old, or so he claimed when they had found him hiding in one of the apartments here in the blocks they first cleared outside the Compound. He looked like he was eight, tops, Jane thought. She'd had a niece that age. Marcy. Jane used to take Marcy to the playground when she baby-sat. She didn't like to wonder about Marcy.

"You okay, Jane?" the boy said, giving her what Marcy had called the stink-eye. "Bad dreams?"

"I'm good, kid. Thanks for the coffee."

Jane poured the coffee from the plastic cup into the metal soup bowl. She swirled the coffee around the bowl, washing the little ring of soup deposits off the walls of the bowl, then tipped the bowl to her lips and drank. Nothing wasted. She ran her finger around the bowl and licked it. She held the cup to her lips and swallowed every trickle.

"Hey Jane," Joey said in a particular tone she had grown to recognize. "Why did the zombie chicken cross the road?"

She gave him her blankest stare, and he hooked his thumbs under his armpits to flap his elbows like wings and squawked: "Grraaaiiinsss!"

Jane chuckled despite her best effort not to, then handed him her empty cup and bowl. She grabbed her backpack and checked her gear.

"Maxwell said you're taking the crew on a food run. I want to go," Joey said.

"Maybe next time. You haven't finished training yet."

"You always say that, but you never even started trying to train me."

She smiled and mussed his hair. "And you always say that. When you figure out why we keep having this conversation, then you'll be ready to start training."

Jane met the recon crew by the Compound gate. She was going into the wild with three others: Willy, Rita, and Johnny.

A former Army Ranger and firefighter, Willy kept his head in scary situations and was used to lugging heavy gear over land and up flights of stairs. In his mid-thirties, he provided the group's muscle, and had proven himself to Jane in some tight spots. Willy was also a crack shot, though they avoided using guns because of the racket.

Rita had been a Pilates trainer; a few years older than Jane, she was in great physical condition, and could outrun any of them. When everyone else cut their hair short to keep it from becoming a Z's finger hold, Rita just shaved her head; Jane at first thought it was extreme, but Moses seemed to like it. Jane had taken to doing the same with hers.

Johnny was Johnny; he didn't talk about himself or much of anything else, but he got jobs done without being told twice. He had been a medic or EMT or something, years before the plague, and the group relied on him for First Aid. Jane couldn't gauge his age, and he never advertised it.

Jane trusted them, and they trusted her. They had done

this kind of pickup-and-run dozens of times, and they had a process that worked for them. They all wore matching gray canvas overalls Jane had liberated from a dry cleaner weeks ago. The long-sleeved outfits helped them blend into the ash and concrete, the thick canvas protected them from scratches and punctures, and they had good zipper pockets for carrying tools, which reduced the loose gear a Z might grab onto.

The problem they had begun to encounter was that each cache of food they found was farther and farther from the Compound. Eventually, they would have to move the Compound closer to the food, or build a secondary compound and a new safe zone around it. Jane looked forward to a day when there were more safe zones than concrete jungle. For now, she'd be satisfied if she could bring everyone back in one piece with enough food to last for a couple of weeks.

At the end of the block, farthest from the Compound, the team climbed a fire escape to a window that they had sealed with a steel door. They unlatched it and entered, closed and latched it behind them, crossed the floor to the other side of the building — the side fronting the wild zone — and opened a similar steel door on the fire escape there. Zs didn't climb ladders, which they'd have to do in order to access the fire escape, so the path should be clear.

The four of them stood on the fire escape and scanned the streets. Rita was the only one with binoculars; she kept them on a cord around her neck, but tucked them inside her coveralls when she wasn't using them. When they all agreed the way was clear, they climbed down and headed west.

They hugged the walls, keeping watch in front and behind as well as the opposing side of the street. Johnny took the point; despite Jane's skills, he had the best nose for lurkers. The buildings they passed at first were marked with Xs and sealed. They knew these places were empty, but soon enough they were in a zone with no marked doors. Jane had bypassed these buildings — many of them abandoned warehouses and empty industrial facilities — in her search for places where people might have left food.

No one spoke. Zs' hearing was almost as acute as their sense of smell; running wasn't the only reason scavenger team members wore high-top sneakers. And the probability of crossing paths with a Z grew with each step they took farther into the wild and closer to the Market Avenue building where Jane had left the food stacked.

The structures grew taller and bunched closer together as they got to Market Avenue. Alleys were narrow and dark where the morning sun hadn't risen high enough to penetrate. The team paused at every alleyway crossing to listen for footsteps, grunts, or moans. Then they hurried past.

One building short of the target, Johnny signaled for them to freeze. He pointed at movement in the opening to an elevated parking garage. Rita checked it with her binoculars. She signaled "two," one mobile and one seated.

They were almost there, Jane thought. They would lose precious time if they tried to circle around the parking garage and back to the apartments, and they were just as likely to run into other Zs along the way. Besides, Jane was more familiar with this route, it was more direct, they were less likely to make a wrong turn in a chase situation, and there was food here they could live off of if they were cut off by a mob.

Using hand signals, they voted, and all agreed they would take down the two Zs between them and the target.

Jane ran ahead. She was the bait. As she passed the garage, the walking Z turned and followed her out onto the sidewalk. The seated one moaned and began shoving itself to its knees, but Willy's machete cracked its skull near the base of the neck and it dropped back down where it had sat.

Johnny and Rita raced past him, closing the gap on the walker following Jane. Rita got there first and whacked the thing in the head with a nine iron. It stumbled and fell face-first on the sidewalk, and brain matter spit from the cracks in its head. It didn't get back up.

Everyone sprinted to catch up with Jane, who was hopping to pull down the ladder at the base of the fire escape they would need to mount. She had hooked it with a length of weighted rope she carried in one pocket for just this use; each of the others had identical ropes in their pockets. The metal clattered and rattled, loud in the silent city, and Rita grimaced, but as they climbed up they saw no sign of the noise having drawn an audience.

In the corridor upstairs, they quickly gathered the cans and boxes Jane had found, stuffing them into backpacks and pockets, zipping them up tight.

"Good haul," Willy said.

Rita grinned. "If there's this much on the other floors, we'll be set for a couple of months."

Johnny didn't speak, just stuffed his backpack and eyed the doors down the corridor. Each of them had an "X" marked in chalk, meaning Jane had cleared them, but Jane could see he remained uneasy.

Jane just nodded; Rita was right, she thought, but there were many more "ifs" hidden in there: If they could get back home alive with this food; if they could return here tomorrow to clear another floor or two; if they didn't get killed doing any of that. She glanced out the window and settled one of the questions right away.

"We're not going back that way," Jane said.

A handful of zombies gathered in the street below. They were reason enough to avoid returning by the same path, but more shuffled out of the parking garage. Jane wondered how they had missed her yesterday, or if they had only been waiting here now because they had caught scent of her having passed this way a day ago. No one really knew how sensitive their noses were, but for creatures that didn't breathe they seemed to be able to sniff out hiding places. Worse still, the long morning shadows of even more Zs were growing in a side street as they approached the intersection and Jane's line of sight.

"Out the other end," Willy said.

Johnny was already there, jimmying the window. They all climbed onto the platform and scanned the streets, gave the all-clear, and descended. Jane took point this time, with Rita, Johnny and Willy following. The ladder squealed as she rode it down to street level, and they wasted no time waiting to see if the din brought any thing to investigate.

They jogged south, away from the crowd on the northeast side of the building, then cut east behind the garage, moving parallel to their original route. George was in Jane's right hand; she wasn't sure when she'd put him there.

That's when they heard the gun shots.

One rang out and echoed. Another.

The four of them skidded to a stop. Willy, a little slower to react than the others, slammed into Johnny and fell onto the concrete. He gritted his teeth, didn't cry out, and the others kept themselves from shushing him.

Another shot echoed among the buildings, and they all tried to identify the source.

"Market," Rita whispered.

Jane nodded. She pointed straight ahead and hand-signaled for the group to move out. "Stay on mission. I'll run to check it, and be right behind you."

Two more shots.

The others hesitated, shared a look. Jane pointed again and they broke into a run. She gripped George tightly and sprinted up the alley back toward Market Avenue and the crowd of Zs they had spotted from the window.

The gunshots were drawing the zombies away from the building and away from her crew, but that didn't mean they would ignore her if they spotted her; she stuck to the deep shadow that remained in the alley as she approached the street, then chanced a quick glance around the corner.

She dropped back into the shadow and processed what

she thought she had seen:

A block further west, a man stood in the middle of the street. He was outfitted in a black body suit of some sort, and he had belts of weapons and hand tools hugging his hips and crossing his chest like bandoleers. Pistols in both gloved hands and more slung in shoulder holsters and hip holsters. He had black knee and shin guards, and black elbow pads over the bodysuit. A black skullcap-style helmet covered his head, and yellow safety goggles covered his eyes.

The zombies swarmed around him, but were not attacking him. They seemed to be unsure what to make of him. They circled him, brushed against him, pawed at him, and though he stepped away from them, he seemed unafraid. There was something else, also, something she wasn't sure she had seen.

She looked around the corner again, pausing a longer moment to watch.

The man had his back to her now. He raised a pistol slowly, placed its muzzle against the nearest zombie skull, and fired. The Z dropped, and the other creatures in the mob turned toward the falling body. A couple of them kneeled and began biting the corpse as if it was fresh, while others fixed their attention on the shooter. One reached toward him, paused, and turned away as if confused, and the ones that had stooped to bite the Z he had shot dropped its bits and began to move away.

The man took several steps, randomly putting himself in a different part of the crowd as Zs milled and wandered. He seemed to be mimicking their motion, blending with them.

And now she clearly saw the other thing she had noticed earlier: A dog was following the man's movements. It was a raggedy mutt, brown and yellow, with ribs showing. It skittered among the zombies, which ignored it, and kept the shooter in its sight.

Jane knew zombies had killed animals during feeding

frenzies. She'd seen it happen. But they tended to view small creatures as even less appetizing than each other. That the dog was staying close to the shooter in this crowd, however, was almost as crazy to her as the man himself.

The man. Jane could see only glimpses of him as her view was obscured by the wandering mob of Zs. He raised the gun, lazily almost, and fired again. As he fired this time, his head turned toward Jane; though his face was covered by the black headpiece and tinted goggles, she was certain he saw her.

Jane darted back into the shadow and gasped. She had been holding her breath. Her heart pounded, and she broke out in a cold sweat. George slipped out of her grip and dangled on his strap.

She listened as the man's guns barked again and again. Closer each time. Closer.

She ran.

**

CHAPTER SEVEN: TARGET FOR DEATH

I gathered weapons from Bill's house and from every corpse and wrecked police car along my route as I walked back into the city that morning. Shrugged into a shoulder holster from a dead detective, took a ball peen hammer from the middle of a street and snugged it in my tool belt. Found a National Guard truck with assault rifles and ammunition intact, and slung the rifle strap over my head; it bounced against my back as I walked. Decided against something looked like a bazooka — a grenade launcher? —that seemed too extreme for my purposes.

I brought Bill's little spear gun, but discarded it after a few unsuccessful test fires. If I couldn't hit slow moving zombies crossing my path, it was useless to me.

I hated using the word "zombie" because it seemed so B-movie. I considered them nearer to "ghouls," creatures of Arabic legend, demons that fed on the living. That thought reminded me of the word "goons." I liked that word.

I took shin and elbow pads from the remains of a man who must have tried to fight his way through the goons;

they would protect me from injuries due to falls better than they had protected him from my less thoughtful kindred. I scavenged a black skullcap helmet from the same motorcycle wreck I had snacked on the day before, hoping it might shield me from bullets to the head. Going where the hunting seemed best meant exposing myself to the possibility of becoming one of the hunted.

Since the beginning of time, nomadic tribes tracked the movements of the wild herds, and logic suggested the goons would follow their senses to where the food could be found in more abundance; I trailed the other predators much like hyenas trailed the leopards, which in turn tracked herds of wildebeests. Only, I intended to kill the cheetahs and pick off the cattle for myself.

I considered, but found it difficult to accept, that goons could be the next step of human evolution. Something lives in my brain. Something animates my body, which otherwise appears to be dead. Something triggers my hunger and compels me to continue existing. Something survived after I died. My plan to kill goons was part of that survival, and perhaps the same decision modern man made when considering the Neanderthal.

When I came upon a mob of goons on Market Avenue, I caught the scent of the humans they had gathered to eat. Unlike the mob, I could tell that the humans had climbed into one of the apartment buildings. I announced my presence loudly in order to attract the attention of my true prey. My camouflage was good, but furthering my plan required for human eyes to see me in action. It wouldn't take long to draw them out, or by careful work to deduce their hiding places.

I spotted the girl peering around the corner, her head covered in a short red bristle like the skin of a Georgia peach. I wondered if it would crunch when I bit into it, and how sweet her brain nectar would taste.

I continued firing for a while in case she chanced another look. When she didn't, I worked my way through the mob toward the corner where I had seen her, but she was long gone by then. A couple of goons that followed me caught her scent, and I used a ball peen hammer to put them down quietly; I didn't want to employ the guns again and keep drawing more mindless feeders to her spoor.

I waited a few minutes, giving the mob time to forget about the noises and disperse, then walked south and tried to pick up her trail. The sensitivity of my nose and ears amazed me, especially when compared to the numbness of my skin. Her scent came stronger to the east and mingled with other aromas; more than one person had passed this way just minutes ago.

I wanted to follow them — the hunger raged for me to follow — but it wouldn't be good for my long term concerns if I caught up to them now and they saw through my disguise. They might even be holed up somewhere to wait and see if I tried to track them. I must be patient, I thought.

Dead men can be quite patient. You may have noticed that we don't hurry.

But I also had to eat. I walked back to Market Avenue and paused in the shadow where the girl had hidden. I watched the goons wander, my mindless cousins, and I wondered again why I, alone, had regained the faculties that none of them had. What set me apart?

Even before I died, inconsistent reports about the plague gave us conflicting information. Initially, the authorities warned us that all zombie bites were deadly, and those who died from a bite would turn into a zombie; later we heard that this wasn't necessarily true. Many of the bitten simply died of the fever and stayed that way, which suggested there might be a genetic factor that rejected the disease or blocked its maturation into whatever caused reanimation.

Might there also be a genetic factor that triggered memory recall and awareness? Would my daughter have reawakened to consciousness if she had been allowed to turn?

It didn't bother me that I would never know the answers to these questions. Watching the goons walking Market Avenue at that moment, I found that the only thing bothering me was the growing desperation at the back of my brain, the throbbing desire that seemed centered in my face rather than my belly. I studied the walkers and hated them because they were inedible, or at least unappetizing. They would not satisfy my hunger.

But my gunfire had caught their attention, and it had brought the girl to investigate; maybe it had caught someone else's ear too. Someone who might be watching this street for my return. There had to be more living people in this city than I had seen so far. More pockets of survivors, or single ones here and there. Surely, someone else had heard my guns.

I focused on the windows of buildings on the far side of the street, which is another thing the goons don't do. They don't look up, typically, unless they hear a loud noise or smell fresh meat. No longer a typical goon, I looked up.

And when I did, I saw a face in a window peering down at the crowd. Six floors up and a block to the west, someone alive intently watched the goons in the street. It appeared to be an older man. Older than me. Gray hair, thin face, wrinkled skin, black frames on his glasses. From the angle of his head, he seemed to be interested in the alley where I hid in the shadow, probably praying that the goon-killer he had spotted would step once more into the light — and likely frightened near to death of what might happen if I did.

When I strode onto the street corner, he instinctively withdrew from the window. He'd been hiding up there for who knows how long, and he didn't want to be seen. Certainly, he was terrified of the goons finding him, but some part of him probably feared being discovered by a ruthless scavenger who would take his food or hurt him. I wondered if he had seen the band of humans pass this way earlier and if he had agonized over whether to call out to them. I imagined that was precisely the case.

I waited, standing in the open, and after several seconds his face returned to the window. He didn't want to be left alone, either. He was too afraid to choose. But when he leaned back into view, I raised my right hand to wave. He hesitated before he waved back, a fluttering of brittle bone and shrunken skin.

He put his face in his hands. Crying. He leaned one palm against the window. I could see him shake as he sobbed.

I imagined his relief at glimpsing what he thought must be another living person, and a friendly one at that. A zombie-slayer. Thinking he was about to be saved. Thinking I would take care of him.

I motioned for him to come down, but he shook his head and waved his hands, seeming to indicate the impossibility of taking that action.

I motioned to him that I could come up.

He trembled; even from this far away, I could tell that his hands shook and his face twitched. As much as he longed for salvation, he remained afraid of being victimized. Finally, he nodded and held up his right index finger.

One moment, he was trying to say. One moment.

He left the window, backing into his apartment. When he returned, he held a sheet of paper to the glass. He had written large numbers on it with a black marker: 615.

I gave him a thumbs-up and crossed the street to the entrance of his building. One of the dead in the street turned to follow me, a skeletal thing in ripped jeans and nothing else. More of that natural herding instinct, possibly. He saw movement and followed.

I put the head of my hammer through his forehead to dissuade him.

Stepping through the buckled front doors, I saw a dead woman shuffling around the lobby. She wore a beige maid's uniform blackened by blood. I still had my hammer in my hand, but when I came close to her I saw a silvery knitting needle protruding from her face; someone had stabbed her in the head, but she had kept going.

I returned the hammer to my tool belt. She studied me for a few seconds with eyes glazed and white, and as she turned away I reached up and snatched out the needle. Black liquid oozed from the wound like oil. She faced me again, stumbled, dropped to her knees, and then expired.

The needle had pierced her skull, but it also had plugged the wound, preventing air from reaching her brain; removing the needle opened the brain — or whatever was left in her head — to the outside air. This confirmed a suspicion I'd heard about before my death, based on the radio reports we got before the power went out, that whatever kept the goons walking was anaerobic in nature. That's why head shots stopped them in their tracks: Opening the brainpan killed it instantly. A small puncture killed it more slowly.

News you could use.

I opened the stairwell door and headed into the darkness, taking my hammer in one hand and my Maglite in the other. I shined the flashlight up the central opening and saw two sets of eyes peer over a railing a few floors above me. I could hear the creatures coming down the steps as I went up.

On the second floor landing, twin little boys scurried forward with white eyes and sunken faces; they had been trapped in the stairwell for weeks or months with no one to eat, and my light confused them. They paused and stood looking at me with a dull curiosity, and I wondered for a moment if they, like me, had awakened from their zombie stupor.

One of them repeatedly clacked his teeth together, like a baby finding its voice. The other laced and unlaced his fingers.

I put the hammer back in my belt and drew a pistol,

shoved it against one boy's temple and angled the barrel so that the bullet would pass through both of their skulls. The shot, horrendous and deafening, echoed up the stairwell and down again. A terrible ambient moan answered as all of the dead people trapped in their apartments or closets or hallways in the structure reacted to the blast.

It sounded like the building itself, crying out its anguish. The groan of Usher collapsing into the loam.

I wondered how quiet that old man must have been to keep them from pounding on his door. I wondered how little he had slept since the end of his world.

It was a long, slow climb in the dark, and I was well and truly alone. At the doorway to the sixth floor, I put away my flashlight again. I pushed open the door, stepped into the dim corridor, and a creature struck me at speed, falling with me to the carpet.

As sunken and hungry as the twins had been, it attacked without first trying to see what kind of thing I was.

What I was, was armed.

Its teeth caught on my shoulder, but failed to puncture the wetsuit. The pistol already in my hand, I pumped a round into the thing's body, knocking it back before its fingernails or biting jaws could inflict any real damage. I got out my hammer and finished it off. Another goon in the hallway hurried to investigate us, but I took it down with a lazy swing of the hammer. It crumpled in a heap that left its ass sticking up in the air, one bloody ear to the floor, as if listening for the rumbled of buffalo herds carried through the earth.

No other goons roamed the corridor, though I heard moans, scratching, and the beating of their limbs on apartment doors as I passed them. At the door marked "615," I stopped. Listened. Sniffed the air. Watched the shadow move at the base of the door and in the circle of the peep hole.

The old man stood just on the other side of the door,

smelling of shit, cat food, and mothballs. My face burned with the madness of the hunger as I listened to the old man breathe heavily, wheezing.

I traded the pistol for the stun gun. I knocked. Shave-and-a-haircut.

"Is it safe?" he said.

"… For the moment."

He unlocked the door and cracked it open, leaving the security chain attached. I stared down at him — the first real test of my disguise.

"I'm here … to rescue you. … How many are with you?"

He seemed unsure, but he slid the chain off and opened the door. "I'm alone. My wife —"

I stepped into his apartment and touched him with the stun gun. He spat, jerked and went down, but he didn't lose consciousness. He squeaked and rattled. He pissed himself and tried to crawl away. He was so thin and frail, I wondered if another zap would stop his heart.

He gasped, "You can't! You can't do that! What you're doing —"

I stomped down hard on his right calf. Heard the bone snap. He screamed this time and flailed his arms. His neighbors moaned in answer. He tried to kick me with his good leg and I stepped back, leveling one of my pistols at him.

He clawed at the air between us, as if bony hands might block my bullets. "No! No, please!"

"Be still, or I shoot you right now."

He stopped kicking. His head lolled back in pain and despair. Snot and tears smeared his face. It was all I could do to keep myself from biting into him.

"I got nothing here!" he cried. "You don't have to do this!"

I got the duct tape out of my tool belt and strapped his wrists together, then hauled him up into the wooden chair he had been sitting in near the window. I taped his hands to one of the chair's arms, and taped his ankles to the chair legs. He howled as I manipulated his broken leg, and the cries of his anguish made the goons in neighboring apartments groan and pound with desire.

"What's your name?" I asked.

He didn't answer. I decided to call him Bob.

"Bob, you're going … to be a big help to me. You're going to teach me … how to keep food alive."

The old man's eyes went wide and crazy. They vibrated and swirled in circles that repeatedly centered on me. His face went red and wet, and a broken whine resonated deep in his throat.

"You can't," he sighed.

"I will."

I took off my tool belt and carefully laid out some of the contents on his coffee table where Bob could see them: folding hacksaw, acetylene torch, bolt cutters.

Bob wept.

**

CHAPTER EIGHT: MEN OF FEAR

Jane ran almost all the way home, pausing only to check cross-streets before making the final turns toward the Compound. She spotted her scavenging crew near the top of the Ashford Building as she ran the last block. They had climbed the fire escape, not pausing to wait for her until they had elevation and safety. Rita turned to scan the street before closing the door, saw Jane, and waved.

Her lungs on fire, Jane made it to the base of the ladder and jumped to drag it down to street level. Mounting the stairs gave her no respite, and Jane's crew waited patiently for her to catch her breath. Still gasping, she told them that they were not going to believe what she had seen.

"A man," she huffed, "in a black … body suit of some kind. Walking among … the Zs and shooting them … one by one."

Jane was right: The looks on their faces made clear that they had trouble believing her. When he heard the report a few minutes later, Maxwell was dubious as well, and he called the whole group of survivors together outside the kitchen to hear Jane's story in detail.

After the scavenger crew checked their new supplies into the pantry, they each got a bottle of rain water and reported in. The rest of the survivors, except for those on watch, heard how they ran across a couple of Zs at the parking garage entrance, how the noises they made then drew a horde of wandering biters, and how, as they made an escape along a parallel route, Jane went back alone to investigate the gunshots.

Jane described the shooter and his actions in as much detail as she could muster, and Maxwell shushed the cross-talk, asking, "Why didn't the Zs attack him?"

Moses spoke up. His gray brows bunched together when he studied a problem. "Could be possible his uniform is coated with something, a chemical or a pheromone maybe, that makes Zs think he's one of them? Maybe the army finally figured something out."

Jane was glad to have Moses around. He was the one who built their rain traps. He had figured out how to run the forklifts and construct their barriers in the streets in the early days. The smartest person in the group, Moses didn't immediately dismiss the unlikely.

"Are you certain the man spotted you?" Maxwell said. "Why did you run away?"

"Well, first off, I'm not fucking Z-proof like he is," she said. "If he was headed my way, and they followed him —"

She didn't need to finish the sentence. They knew what she meant.

"It just doesn't make sense," Maxwell said.

Moses laughed. "We're living in the goddamned Z-pocalypse. The dead walk the earth. What part of that makes sense to you?"

But the seed of doubt had been planted, and Jane looked around the group at all the uncertain faces and felt like she could read their minds. They wondered if they could trust her. Wondered if she was losing it. Wouldn't be the first time one of the group cracked. They probably expected her to take off over the fence by herself and never come back; that's what the last crazy person in the camp had done. They were frightened for her and of her.

The worst thing, to Jane, was the doubt in Maxwell's eyes.

"We all heard the shots," Willy offered. "We didn't see this superhero dude, though. I mean, it could have been a loon who was just trying to take some of them with him. Maybe you just didn't see them attack."

"What I saw was them not attack," Jane said. "Whatever. He's out there. He's killing Zs, and he's not afraid of them. We'll see him again. You'll see him."

She got up and went back into the kitchen, grabbed a box of Honey Nut Cheerios she had brought back from the food run. She opened the top and tipped the box up, pouring her mouth full. She stood in the doorway and chewed as the others looked at her, agape.

Bunch of mouth breathers, she thought. She hoped to see their faces when they all saw the gunman for themselves.

But as Jane stared back, she realized some of them probably couldn't believe that, on top of her wild gunslinger story, she just broke one of their cardinal rules by taking food from storage without dividing it. She saw see it on their faces. Surprise. Disbelief. Fear.

Just further proof Jane was finally going over the edge, making up this mad tale of a zombie-proof cowboy and then brazenly raiding their supplies. After all she'd done for them, Jane thought, all the food she'd found, all the times she'd risked her life, now they doubted her word, or her right to eat any damn box of cereal she wanted.

Jane set her jaw, stared them down, and walked away with the cereal box. Maxwell shook his head when she passed. Nobody tried to stop her.

Joey ran up and matched Jane's speed, taking two steps for each one she took. She didn't slow down to go easy on him, stalking right past the school bus and deeper into the junkyard.

"Hey Jane," he said. "What did the zombie say to the girl next door?"

She was not in the mood for him. Jane glared at him without breaking stride. "Don't bother me," she said.

"Wrong. He said, 'Will you be my ghoul-friend?' "

Jane stopped walking and looked down at the boy. It was difficult to stay mad with him, but she was going to try.

"Jane, I believe you," Joey said. "I think something's happening out there. Maybe somebody has worked out how to fight them. Maybe they'll be coming to rescue us soon, and they'll bring all of us a zombie-proof suit."

She shook her head. Joey still believed they would be saved, she thought. He still had faith that some greater power would win the day, and the world that had died in flames and terror would come back. Cable TV. Video games. The Internet. Comic books. All would be restored.

Jane tipped the cereal box high and filled her mouth again. As she chewed, she closed the lid. She handed the box to Joey. He reached to stuff his hand inside, but she placed her fingers over the flaps.

"Go put that back in the pantry for me," she said. "It was wrong of me to take it."

"It's okay, Jane," he said. "You had a rough day. You earned it."

She shook her head. It was not okay. She was not okay. Everyone still breathing was having a rough day.

Jane gave Joey the hand signal to head out, and he did. She went in the other direction and wandered among the stacks of flattened cars, scattered pieces of chrome detailing and chunks of broken plastic. Like them, she felt like she had been crushed and left to rot, but at least she still could get up and go.

**

CHAPTER NINE: MEASURES FOR A COFFIN

Bob didn't last nearly as long as I would have liked. Not long at all, to be perfectly honest about it. But I really tried to give him a shot at living through the early stages of the experiment.

First I gave the old man two of the Hydrocodone tablets from my belt pouch, the ones left over from my wife's post-surgery prescription. She didn't like taking pain medicine, so I had most of a bottle remaining. They were more than a year old, but ought to have worked. It would be simple enough to get more when those ran out; surely not all the pharmacies had been raided for drugs already. The idea here, though, was to blunt Bob's pain as much as possible so he didn't just die on me outright.

Plus, I was interested to see if I could get a buzz off of him.

It's called *science*.

I pushed the pills into his mouth, but he was dry, so I took the pills off his tongue and looked for something with which he could wash them down. Stagnant water pooled under maggots squirming in his kitchen sink. I filled a dirty cup, and poured the water into his mouth, holding his jaw to force him to swallow. He coughed and water squirted from the corners of his lips, but he swallowed.

While I waited for the drug to take effect, I looked around the apartment. Empty cat food tins had turned black in the sink, which explained the man's scent. I wondered if he might taste of tuna. Not much else was left in the place. It looked like he had been without fresh water for a while.

A photo of him and an old woman sat on the window sill where he had watched the street. A woman's clothes were hanging in half of the closet. His wife was not here; I wondered if she had gone out to try to find help or supplies and had never returned. Maybe she was one of the sexless goons I had dropped in the hallway.

Empty pill bottles lay scattered on the bathroom counter; I checked to see if they would have been useful to me, but they had contained only blood pressure and cholesterol medications.

I discovered what was left of their cat in the bathtub, a pile of white bones and bits of fur beside a butcher knife. Bob had eaten it raw. Still, it was no wonder the man didn't go out looking for food, what with his birds-eye view of the carnage on the street, the not-so-dead people stalking the corridor, and the sound of other neighbors scratching at the walls between their apartments.

He must have seen me as a savior. Must have looked down on my activity in the street, the goons falling to my hail of bullets, and rejoiced. Others would make the same mistake, if I was careful on the set-up. Build their trust, dangle a chance of escape from the horde, and lead them to the slaughter. They would come to me. Desperate people would be more susceptible to buying into the fairy tale.

I took a sheet from the bed and returned to the living area. Removed my headpiece and gloves, and wrapped the sheet over my wetsuit before I started cutting on him. I didn't want to get anything on the suit if I could help it. The smell of fresh blood would draw walkers to me in the street, and the sight of dried blood on my suit would make living humans distrustful.

I had waited for what seemed like a very long time, thinking the drug would need a while to take effect. But honestly, he was moaning incoherently from the beginning, so I didn't know if he was ready or not.

That's why I said, "Ready or not, here I go."

I was careful to cut away only a small portion to start — I began with the foot on his broken leg, severing it at the ankle — then used the torch to cauterize the stump. I didn't want him to bleed to death. He passed out from the pain or possibly the drug — more likely, the pain — before I had made any real progress on the cutting.

I chewed on the foot as I tried shaking him awake, but found that he had stopped breathing at all, and I couldn't very well apply CPR.

I made a mental note to find an ambulance, gather a portable defibrillator and plastic ambu-bag in case this sort of thing proved to be a common reaction.

Meanwhile, I was back to square one. I should have been feeling frustration, disappointment. Any number of other emotions. Even anger. But my reaction was, at best, purely clinical.

I believe Bob might have lived through a slow dissection as I had planned, if not for the fact that he was old and weak, malnourished and already suffering from a heart condition. He'd been trapped here for weeks, at least, with access to neither food nor his regular medication. Through his open pajama shirt, I could see the faded white scar of a heart surgery from years ago bifurcating his chest, so it was inevitable that he was going to die, even without my coaxing him along.

I did wish that he had lasted longer, so I could have gotten a better feel for the death threshold. I supposed for some, it would be pain that caused them to die, and for others it would be loss of blood. Some might expire from sheer terror. I hadn't counted on frailty making my first attempt such an utter failure.

Now I ate the meat off of Bob's bony foot and moaned despite myself. The noise was involuntary; when I thought about it later, I couldn't pinpoint if it was a sign of satisfaction or anguish. All I knew at the moment was that this leathery old foot was delicious, and it made me want more. I put down the foot and chose a meaty piece of thigh, got on my knees and bit into it. The blood, though already settling, was thin and provided a wonderful gush of warmth down my throat. I felt ravenous, and the blood made me crazy. I ate and ate.

After a while, I sat back and wiped my face on the sheet. I stood and looked around. On the street, the shadows had disappeared. The sun was directly overhead. The goons still bunched across the way and wandered in aimless circles, a moving obstacle that would keep the girl and her people from returning for more food if they remained mobile.

At least now that I had spotted the girl and sniffed out her companions, I knew there were living people in the area. They were organized and scouting these buildings for food to lug back to a safe place, a sanctuary. It would probably be within no more than a few blocks of here, where other hungry people would be waiting; if not, the small group I had rousted would have just holed up where the food was to ride it out until they had to seek another source. Clearly, they were working for a larger band. They would be somewhere to the east, as that was the direction they had run, though that left quite a bit of ground to cover and didn't allow for them taking a circuitous route to throw off pursuit.

I would have to reconnoiter. Gather supplies and settle in here with some reasonably fresh food, then wait for the group to return. They would be curious to find me, and no doubt they had more of their own food to gather in the building across the way; I could help them by clearing more of the goons.

I pulled my hood back on, secured my glasses, put on my gloves. Gathered my tools and checked my weapons. Went back downstairs and found Rocky waiting in the lobby, gnawing what was left of the goon maid I had put down. He didn't wag his tail, but when I told him to heel, he followed me.

**

Maxwell found Jane in the graveyard, the farthest corner of the Compound away from their living area. Here, among rotting upholstery and rusting metal frames, they buried their dead and their own waste — a hell of a job, as tractor wheels and piles of metal moved here and there over the years had packed the earth as hard as concrete.

Even so, a fresh hole opened in the ground, and Jane sat atop of a pile of dirt by the hole, resting a pointed shovel on her shoulder. Sweat dripped from her face and arms. She breathed raggedly; Maxwell imagined she had taken to the job with all of the energy her anger could generate.

"So who's the hole for?" he said.

"Whoever needs it. Nobody's been out here in a while to dig a new one, and the john needs to be emptied."

He leaned against the frame of an old pickup and crossed his arms. "You get all that out of your system?"

"I'm finished with this hole, if that's what you mean."

Maxwell grunted. "You know what I mean. I need to know if you're going to be okay, because if you're losing it —"

"Don't worry about me." Jane stood, leaned on the shovel, pointed two fingers of her free hand at Maxwell. "I know what I saw, and you'll all know it too, soon enough. Guy like that will be hard to miss. Next time we go on a run —"

"That's the thing, Jane. I appreciate all you did, locating the building and finding the food. Taking the team there and getting everyone back safe. But the others can handle the next run, I think. They can —"

Jane tossed the shovel down. She clasped her hands and squeezed her anger between them, growling high in her throat. Maxwell imagined she pictured his neck between her fingers.

"Don't act like a child, Jane."

Jane took a breath. "I'm nobody's child," she said, and it was how calmly she said it that gave Maxwell pause.

"Okay. But Willy and the others can clear another couple of floors and tote the grub back," he said. "You need to take a day or two and rest up. You'll be ready to go back out again soon."

Jane grimaced at him. "Don't pretend you're doing me a favor."

"Would you rather I say this is punishment for stealing from the pantry? That was not cool, Jane, choking back that cereal it in front of everyone like —"

"Like what? Like it was mine? Like I found it? How many of them have gone out there to scavenge supplies? They sit here on their asses, nice and safe, and wait for me to feed them. Fucking sheep."

"Nobody asked you to be the one. You took that on yourself. Now I'm asking you to stand down for a couple of days."

"Asking?"

Maxwell huffed. "Telling you, then. Get some rack time. Read a book or something. Take a turn at watch duty."

Jane put her fingers in her hair and pulled.

Maxwell picked up the shovel and dropped it at her feet. "Or you could just dig some more holes," he said. "You're pretty good at that, too."

**

CHAPTER TEN: THE DISAPPEARING LADY

Jane moved into the quiet city without a backward glance at the junkyard. She left while the others ate their supper, giving the high sign to the watchers even as she knew they would hurry report her to Maxwell at the first chance. She didn't care that the sun was low, that night would probably catch her in the jungle lands. The digital camera in her front pocket would explain everything when she returned to them. And she fully intended to do so; she wasn't ready to go into a fresh hole yet.

She found the carnage at the corner of Market Street impressive, dozens of Zs spread like trees felled by an explosion in their midst. Recently dispatched and truly dead, as the flies had set in to feast and lay eggs. Jane tried to discern the gunslinger's path, searched for evidence of his boot prints in the black blood coagulating on the pavement, but wherever he had stepped was now obscured by the seeping head wounds.

"Where are you, cowboy?" Jane said, then bit her lip. She knew better than to speak in the empty streets, where voices carried like dinner bells on the dead air.

He must be nearby still, she thought. The gunslinger. The super-hero. Jane wondered what sort of man would brave the zombie infestation like that, then reconsidered her own bravery — or stupidity; at least the gunman seemed to be Z-proof.

Jane scanned each cross-street for signs of recent kills as much as for walking corpses, hoping to discover enough of a trail to lead her wherever the gunman might be holed up for the night. If she could find him, she thought, maybe she could persuade him to help the Compound. The train of thought brought her anger to the forefront again, and she tried to focus on the hunt.

She hoped he wouldn't just shoot her if he saw her; hoped he wouldn't fear losing his zombie-proof uniform or whatever his charm against Zs might be. Jane touched the camera through the fabric of her coveralls and reminded herself that she only needed a photo or two of the gunman in action.

Jane paused outside a motorcyclists' shop off Market Avenue to settle her mind and catch her breath. She hadn't seen a Z all afternoon, except for the ones her quarry had left lying in the street. It was like the man was trying to clear the city all alone, a one man army corps. But her nerves wouldn't stop jumping at every shadow, and she knew that was a bad sign. She needed to calm down, catch her breath, get her head on straight again.

She rested on the shop's wooden window sill, her backpack cushioning her against the intact plate glass, and took a swig from her canteen. The street was devoid of movement, except for breezes blowing trash into random swirls. She watched a plastic shopping bag float over the roof of a burned-out car. The sky above was deep blue, shading toward purple, cloudless, an infinite sea.

The glass behind her made a loud *crack*.

Jane spun to see a dead man's face and hands pressed against the window inside the store. He appeared dry, skeletal, but his tongue and lips left a slime trail on the pane as he tried to eat her through the glass. Jane almost struck him through the window, but she knew the noise of smashing glass would draw attention like crashing cymbals. Instead, she moved to the shop door, letting the Z follow her.

He met her at the door, like a disheveled greeter, still wearing his company vest with its buttons and flair. His nametag read, "Lester." He pushed against the safety glass door, but never thought to turn the knob.

Jane shook George loose and swung the hatchet into her right hand. She steadied herself, then reached for the knob with her left. Lester didn't watch her movement; he had eyes only for the bigger picture, and his teeth snapped together in anticipation. Jane stepped to the side so the door would open outward between her and Lester, and she turned the knob. Lester's weight pushed the door wide, and Jane snatched it back even faster. Lester fell forward, face-first onto the sidewalk.

"Easy-peasy," Jane said.

Jane planted George in the back of Lester's head and stepped over him, entering the shop. She kicked Lester's legs to the side and closed the door behind her. Never leave doors open, even if it's your exit, she reminded herself.

She stood inside the dark shop and listened. No hush of feet sliding on the tile floor whispered to her from the shadows. No moan or wheeze of a lifeless thing drawing air. No crunch or smash of items falling over as a Z bumped along the aisles. Just silence, like a dead world ought to sound, she thought, and with it came a lingering smell of old, dried rot.

The store appeared to be more or less intact, which Jane realized she should have considered when she first saw its big windows unbroken. The place specialized in leather goods, helmets, boots, jewelry, and other gear related to motorcycles, so it had not been an immediate target for people looking for weapons or food. Jane walked the aisles in wonder, imagining herself as a shopper on an afternoon when the lights had gone out. Any minute, they'd come back and she could have Lester ring up her order. Then she recalled an old *Twilight Zone* episode about a woman trapped in a department store after closing time, when the mannequins came to life. The memory made her wonder if Lester used to work here, or if he only took on a semblance of life after closing time.

Jane shook her head at her own weird musings.

She worked her way to the rear of the shop, where the fading sunlight didn't penetrate. The pen light in her pocket wasn't much better, barely cutting a pinpoint through the darkness, and the smell of something rotten grew with each step. Jane backed out of the shadow, retracing her route to an aisle with lanterns and flashlights arranged in neat stacks and rows for the biker planning a bit of roadside camping. She picked out a boxy 9-volt light, and grinned when it switched on, shining a white beam that illuminated the store like a searchlight.

Jane never would have found this place, so far off her previous route, unless she had been trying to find the cowboy. And she would have walked right past it, if not for Lester.

"Thanks, Lester," she said.

The back of the store consisted of an open stockroom with a high ceiling and pallets of boxed merchandise in neat rows, a small office area, rest rooms, and an employee lounge with a microwave, refrigerator, drink and snack machines, and small lockers. The stink came from this room, where Lester must have crawled away to die; she found blood, vomit, and skin dried to the floor. There were no windows, even at the back of the stockroom.

Jane picked up a metal folding chair and smashed the snack machine's glass front, then dumped the bags of chips, M&Ms, cookies, Funyuns, crackers, Juicy Fruit gum, and Snickers in her backpack. She planned to bring the salvage team back with her soon to get the rest, and raid the soda machine as well.

On her way out again, Jane spotted racks of one-piece racing suits, with reinforced knees and elbows, and stretch material in the underarms and crotch. She studied the suits in the dark, trying to compare them in her memory to the outfit she had seen the gunslinger wearing that morning. His was more like a wetsuit, she decided, and like Moses suggested, it was most likely coated with some kind of chemical or pheromone to keep the Zs confused.

But this racing suit looked durable. Fashioned from black leather with rubberized joint pads, it was meant to protect a racer from road rash. She fingered the material, tried to gauge how well it would shield her from biters. Had to be better than a canvas jumpsuit alone, she thought, and she picked out one her size.

Jane sat on the floor and yanked off her sneakers, then stripped out of her coveralls in the dark, all at once more vulnerable than she could remember feeling since the end of the world. The silence in the store suddenly seemed ominous. Jane put her back to a wall and climbed into the racing suit. She found a mirror and looked at herself, and she felt like a skinny super-hero.

But was she? She had run off again, putting herself in danger just to prove a point to Maxwell. Not very heroic. Selfish — stupid, even.

The anger returned, directed at herself this time, and Jane resolved to bring the others back here as soon as feasible and grab all of them some racing gear. In the meantime, she had to make it home before dark without standing out against the landscape, so she put her jumpsuit back on over the leathers. The combination fit too tight. The two outfits catching on one another restricted her movement, but Jane decided she could wear larger coveralls next time. She slipped into her sneakers and tied them tight, and turned off the flashlight as she hurried to the front door.

She rounded a display near the front register and froze.

A crowd of window shoppers had gathered. Hungry ones.

Jane slowly melted into a crouch, counting seven Zs at the glass and four more approaching on the street behind them. She couldn't hear them through the thick plate until they pressed their faces and gnarled fingers against the window, then their sounds transferred through as weird hums and squeaks.

Drawn by her scent, or the noise she made killing Lester, or perhaps even the gunfire earlier this morning echoing through the concrete canyons. Perhaps they saw their own reflections in the window and mistook the images for food; Jane had seen it happen many times. She had used it as a diversion in the past, but now she silently cursed at the window for keeping them interested and blocking her escape.

As Jane watched, still others joined the crowd, pushing against one another for a better position. She knew if they spotted her inside, the crush of their effort would finally bring the glass down and they would swarm over one another to get to her.

The rear exit, then. Maybe the alley would be clear. Or maybe there was a way up to the roof from indoors that she hadn't seen earlier; "climb" was the first rule when things turned to shit in the Z-pocalypse.

Jane edged back, bumped a display rack, and spun to catch it as it tipped.

She missed. The metal stand crashed into a hanging shelf of chrome gear, and like dominoes tumbling, it collapsed onto lower shelves that smashed and fell beneath it.

Now she heard the Zs clearly. The racket coming from the shop had them convinced food was hiding there. They moaned loudly, and even more of them pressed against the window and the door. Jane heard the glass pop and crackle, and she turned to run.

She flew down the aisles and through the swinging

double doors into the stockroom. Waved the flashlight in search of something she could use to block the doors. The handles of a pallet jack rose beside a neat stack of boxes, and she gave the handles two quick pumps to raise the flat, then yanked on it with all her strength. It creaked and moved, then stopped.

Glass shattered at the front of the store, and the dead called out to her.

Jane pumped the handles two more times, pushed, then pulled, and the heavy stack rolled free. She turned and shoved it against the doors, which swung both ways, but she pressed the handle to drop the stack, hoping the horde would try to push, pile up against each other, and not accidentally pull the doors back to open them.

She heard them coming, judging their distance by the uproar of them thrashing through the glass, climbing over each other, tripping on fallen merchandise and display racks. Too close already.

The flashlight probed around the room, pointing out two standard steel doors and a wide metal garage door between them for unloading delivery trucks. Jane tried the nearest door, but it was padlocked. The second door opened to a small chamber housing a device for crushing cardboard boxes. An exterior door in this room also was padlocked.

She heard the groans, the thumping of numb hands and bodies against the swinging stockroom doors behind her. She didn't dare shine the light in that direction until she tried the garage door.

A throw-bolt and a cotter pin held it shut.

The crash of boxes overturning brought her light around involuntarily, and she saw the bodies scrambling over the pallet, one swinging door opened, blocked with other bodies trying to fit through all at once.

Jane pulled the cotter pin, yanked the bolt, threw up the rolling garage door.

A dozen or more Zs standing in the alley turned to face

her, confused by the moans and thrashing sounds echoing from the other side of the building.

Jane smashed the big flashlight into the nearest Z, and it fell into two others, sinking all three onto the pavement. The ones further back leaned in and slouched toward Jane, one tripping across the fallen three, but the others closing fast.

Jane sprinted for the open street at the far end of the alley, and just as she felt she might outrun her slow pursuers, she glimpsed the first of the crowd turning the corner to block her way. She skidded to a stop, looked all around.

Telephone pole.

An old wooden phone pole stood crookedly in the alley. It looked as if it hadn't been in use for a long time, but it still had the steel L-bolts in both sides for ease of climbing. No lines ran to it, and it hugged the brick of an adjacent building, but it was her only choice.

Jane grabbed a set of the bolts and hauled herself up. She got her feet on the lower bolts and climbed.

The Zs gathered below, glaring up at her and groaning their displeasure. She felt a rush of relief once again that none of them could remember how to climb.

She gripped the bolts, about twenty feet in the air now, and wondered what she would do next. No handholds, pipes, or ledges jutted from the tall building beside the pole. The nearest window access hung about twenty feet to her right, much farther than she could hope to leap.

Below, the crowd continued to grow as the Zs from inside the store joined the ones Jane had found in the alley, and more from the street beyond answered their moaning herd. They pressed in on one another, crushing and trampling each other in their single minded desperation to reach Jane's pole. Those closest to it grasped the wood and pulled or pushed as the inclination struck them.

The pole creaked and cracked. It shifted, and Jane's left hand slipped. She hugged the rough wood with her knees and felt her leg muscles straining as she whipped her hand back to grab on once again.

She looked down.

One of the Zs stood absolutely still in the shambling horde. He remained silent while the others milled and wheezed. He looked up at Jane, a calm center in the mass of grasping creatures. Pale eyes peered from a face nearly stripped of flesh. His jaw clamped shut. Quiet. Watching. Considering the situation.

Jane's gut went cold and she broke out in a sweat, making her fingers all the more slick on the rusted metal bolts. She grabbed on, climbed higher. Near the top of the pole, 40 feet up but no closer to an escape, she looked down again.

The quiet Z had moved to the base of the pole, persistently pushing other zombies aside. He glowered up at Jane. Reached for the lowest of the L-bolts. Took hold of it in his rubbery hand and tried to pull himself up, stripping skin from his fingers.

"Holy fuck," Jane said.

The Z couldn't get enough clearance from the press of hungry moaners to drag himself above the crush of the crowd. He shoved them aside and reached up again, but the mob refilled the space, pushing against the pole, which made a second, louder popping noise and shifted farther to one side.

Jane held on, mind racing, heart pounding. She scanned the buildings around her, hoping for a miracle. Again, she noted the broken window nearly twenty feet away, but as she had climbed to the pinnacle of the post, it was now below her as well. She did a quick calculation and realized that, if the pole continued to tip without falling altogether, and if she could hang on as it moved, then she would pass very close to the window. Perhaps close enough to grab the sill.

The glass shards in the frame would hurt her, and she hated to think what kind of mob her spilled blood could draw. But she saw no other choice.

The pole wobbled, and Jane looked down, right into the staring eyes of the one quiet zombie in the crowd. She recognized the expression on his emaciated face — not the brainless hunger of the mob, but rather the sparkle of an angry intelligence. His eyes tracked to the window, and she knew he had considered the possibility that she might make her escape there.

Jane trembled. Then she cursed herself. She tried throwing her weight to the right, pulling at the phone pole, pushing against the wall, forcing the pole to move.

Maybe it would fall all at once, killing her on impact before the Zs could rend her flesh. She grimaced at the realization that might be her best hope.

The pole wobbled again and tipped at almost a sixty-degree angle from the street, stopping with a sudden jerk that made Jane bite her lip. She hugged the wood desperately, catching thick splinters in her fingers and the palms of her hands. She hooked her ankles on the lower footholds as her weight shifted toward the earth, which was now off to her side. She stared at the window, elated for a moment that she seemed to be inching toward it perfectly.

Then a Z stuck its head out the shattered glass, drawn from wherever it had lurked within the building to investigate the commotion of the excited horde. It didn't see Jane hanging so close above it, as it was fascinated by the noises below. Its long, stringy hair and clothing the dingy brown of dried bodily fluids kept Jane from distinguishing its gender.

Jane tried to look over her shoulder and spot the quiet Z in the crowd, but she couldn't see from this angle. She reached around the high side of the pole with her left arm, wrapped her left leg around and between the pole and the brick wall, and anchored her knee in one of the climbing bolts. She got enough of a grip to pull herself to the upward-facing edge of the post, just as the pole began to dip downward again.

As it fell, Jane's left leg dragged along the brick and mortar of the wall, grinding her knee between the pole and the building. She grunted and yelled in pain, and the zombie in the window turned to look up at her just as the pole crossed the top of the sill.

The pole struck the Z on the shoulder, jammed it down against the sill, and wedged it there. It struggled helplessly, facing the mob below and swinging its arms in wide, useless circles. Jane felt its movements causing the pole to shift, and she knew she had only seconds to dismount. She crawled over the squirming corpse, and threw herself into the dark room behind the Z. The force of her leap caused the pole to fall away from the building into the crowd below, ripping the Z's upper body away from the legs and pelvis.

Jane landed on her hurt knee and crumpled into a ball on the floor, momentarily blind with pain. She pushed herself to one side — *keep moving!* — whipped George into her right hand, came upright, and scanned the room for attackers. Sweat streamed into her eyes, burning them, blurring her vision. She wiped her face on her sleeve, and the sleeve came away bloody. Realized she hit her head when she landed.

Jane saw the little room, bare walls and wooden floors, a closed door, and felt the hot blood rush through her face in the relief of knowing the room was empty except for herself and the lower half of the Z that had come to the window. Its backbone extended above the torn meat of its abdomen like an antenna and twitched randomly before the legs folded to the floor.

Jane crawled to the window, pulled herself up, and peeked over the edge of the sill.

The mob had scattered. Some already wandered away in their confusion. The fallen pole trapped some of them, and put others down permanently. Jane couldn't be sure if one of the crawling half-bodies below belonged to the window Z. And she saw no sign of the quiet one that had tried to follow her up the pole. None of them looked up now, having forgotten she was even there.

Jane drooped against the wall beside the lower half of the Z, and her vision blurred again. Her heart thumped loudly in her ears, so loud that she couldn't hear the rabble outside or any noises inside the building. She tried to listen, staring at the closed door, wondering what lurked on the other side, or what might even now be approaching and have enough mind to know to turn the knob.

Jane gripped her bum knee and slumped onto the floor away from the half-corpse. The sun was setting, and she would be in total darkness soon, in a building surrounded by Zs, one of whom might be almost as smart as her. She needed to get up and find a way out. But her pain and fatigue proved too much.

Jane blacked out, clutching George in one hand and her throbbing knee in the other.

**

CHAPTER ELEVEN: THE THING THAT PURSUED

I set up shop in Bob's apartment. I ate cold meat and watched the street below, waiting for the scavengers to return. Rocky sat outside in the hallway. He wouldn't go into the old man's place with me, but he was okay chewing on the dry dead things in the corridor.

I will never understand dogs.

I wondered if the humans would continue stripping groceries and supplies from the building across the street, or if they were finished over there and would turn their attention to this building. Maybe they would come in and find me. Maybe I would kill a few before they killed me for good and all. The prospect of ending this existence didn't frighten me, but I preferred to plan for survival.

During the night, I gathered a half-dozen digital "trap" cameras from the home security store down the street and set them up on nearby corners. Tried to hide them behind phone poles, inside broken electrical boxes, or mangled wrecks. The cameras ran on batteries, were tripped by motion and took infrared photos. Unlike normal hunting trap cameras, they used a black infrared

LED rather than a flash, so the subject was unlikely to be disturbed in action or see the camera.

The idea was to narrow down the direction from which the humans were coming. Once I got a hit, I'd move the cameras further along their path. Slowly, step by step, I would discover their origins. I needed to find them first. Figure out their patterns. When they looked for food. How many they sent out. That kind of thing. Then I would set myself up as a source of supplies for them; they wouldn't have to risk coming out of their sanctuary because their unseen friend in the city was feeding them. I could fatten them up, make them slow and lazy. Get into their heads and make them stupid.

Finally, I would convince them to come out to me one at a time somehow; offer them something they dreamed about, a chance to make it to a place where the goons had been cleared altogether.

Hope. I could use their hunger and their dreams against them. And one at a time, I would lead them to my dinner table.

I was surprised on that first day after the woman saw me. I hadn't really expected the humans to return again so soon, but they no doubt wanted to see if I was around or if I had left some evidence of my work. Sure. They wanted to know if the young woman who spotted me had been telling the truth. The girl with the peach fuzz head.

I couldn't be certain from the distance, but I didn't think I saw her among the small group. They came out of the alley where she had watched me, and they studied the bodies of the goons in the street for a long time before edging into the open.

I shot a bunch of dead people yesterday. They piled on top of each other where they fell. I knew the sight would be impressive.

I stood far back from Bob's viewing window behind a folding privacy curtain, using binoculars to watch the street; I knew they wouldn't see me even when they scanned the windows of the buildings all around them. I didn't flinch when they looked my way.

Two men and one woman — not a red-head, her fuzz was brown. The woman used a small digital camera to shoot video of the carnage in the street. She came prepared to take back proof of whatever they found. One of the men established where I had stood and shot — he actually mimicked what he believed would have been my stance and firing positions, pointing out where the bodies fell for the sake of the camera.

They moved on to the building they had explored the day before, taking only a few minutes to climb a fire-escape to one of the top floors. And they came back out minutes later, backpacks bulging with supplies they must have cached yesterday. They descended the same fire escape and briefly wandered out of my view, then returned the way they had come, disappearing into the alley shadow.

I didn't move. I continued to watch.

Something stirred in the alley. Something reflected off metal in the shadow.

I continued to stand perfectly still and observe. After a while, with nothing else happening, I still continued to stand perfectly still and observe.

I don't get tired. I don't get bored.

Sometime later, I decided they had left the area. I made my way downstairs, letting the dog go ahead of me. Rocky trotted out of the lobby onto the street and froze in place, sniffing the air. I waited by the broken doors and watched the street. The dog snuffled around in circles, catching the same scent I was picking up now: Fresh food, though admittedly the dog probably didn't think of them in that way. I could smell the recent passage of humans, and I followed the scent.

At the first corner along the alley, I retrieved the trap camera and checked it for images. It had taken four shots of the trio as they passed the corner, hunched over, weapons in hand. I cleared the memory and put the camera in a belt pouch, then continued in the direction the scent led me, which was also the direction the camera had indicated they came from. The dog paralleled me on the opposite sidewalk.

At the next corner, I checked the next camera. Three more images. The pictures jibed with my sense of smell, and I continued on the trail, dropping the second camera in my pouch. Halfway along the block, the stench of fresh bleach blanked my nose; the humans must have spread it along their path to discourage pursuit.

Rocky actually got too much of a snort and whined, then scrubbed his snout against the pavement. It was the first sound he had made in days.

A goon shuffled out from between two wrecked cars, drawn by my movement and the dog's whining. It was gaunt and tattered, naked, with burn scars covering most of its body. I couldn't tell if it had been male or female. I ignored it and moved along to the next corner and the next camera, which I had set in the strut of a bus stop bench.

More images of the three scavengers. They looked delicious in their gray coveralls. However, my sense of smell had not cleared; bleach really did a number on our noses, and while I no longer considered myself a mere goon, I remained a zombie. I would have to trust to the cameras.

The goon followed me, thinking I was on the trail of food, or perhaps even picking up the scent I had lost; I was moving this way, his thinking seemed to indicate, so this was the way to move. I waited to see if it had caught the humans' trail, but it stood quietly beside me, looking around randomly at the ground. I half expected it to ask me the time or take a seat and wait for the next bus. It never made eye contact.

I took the hammer off my tool belt and knocked a hole in its head.

At the next corner, though, my luck ran out. The

humans had not come this way. I had one more camera to retrieve, another block along the way; it, too, was empty. I doubled back to the last place I had captured an image of them and considered the options. I reset that camera, and began placing the others along other potential pathways, one a block south, one a block further west, then another south and another west. I marked the locations on the city map I carried in another pocket.

I was returning to my perch in Bob's apartment when I heard the slap of bare feet on pavement, rebounding from the high walls of the silent city. The runner was not being careful or quiet, which meant he was being chased. The breeze was not in my favor, so I had yet to get a scent. I dropped back into the nearest doorway and crouched down, easing a pistol out of its holster and watching.

I grabbed up some trash and newspapers the wind had deposited in the doorway, and used it to cover myself. Just another corpse in the street, now. The perfect camouflage.

Rocky jogged off and found his own place to hide.

A woman stopped at the intersection to my north. She was naked except for a muddy windbreaker she had wrapped around her shoulders. Her bones pressed against pale skin marked with bruises and welts. Short hair matted down, the color of mud. Left eye blackened and swollen. When the breeze shifted, I caught the tang of her blood on the air and felt my brain catch fire.

She was poorly fed and had been mistreated, and I wanted so badly to save her. For myself.

She hesitated at the corner and spun around in the middle of the street, lost and terrified. She looked behind her, then glanced around for a direction to run. I thought she looked right at me, but it's possible her eyesight was poor or obscured by injury.

She ran on, headed south, and I let her pass. I wanted to see what pursued her, because I heard no moaning goons. I tried to push further back into the doorway, but it was no good. I slumped lower and slid out a second pistol.

A minute later, a man eased into view at the corner. He wore desert fatigues, polarized sunglasses, and combat boots, and he carried an assault rifle with a homemade noise suppressor over the barrel. His head was shaved, and the black swirl of tribal tattoos marked his arms and neck. He moved in a crouch, much like the scavengers I had photographed, but he wasn't searching for canned food.

He was hunting — hunting the woman.

He scanned right past me and continued through the intersection, still on the trail of the woman. I waited until his footfalls had receded to get back on my feet, then I peered around the corner. I saw him kneeling in the street about half a block away, examining something on the pavement. Probably a blood spatter from his fleeing prey.

I aimed at his back, but knew I wouldn't be able to hit him from here. I would have to get closer somehow.

As I returned to the doorway where I had been hiding, I glanced around for the dog, but Rocky was nowhere to be seen. I wondered if he was more afraid of humans now than of goons; I remembered the cat carcass in Bob's apartment and it occurred to me that eating domestic animals must have become common in recent weeks. Rocky was smart. He'd learned that humans couldn't be trusted.

I pushed open the building's front door. It creaked, and moans answered the sound. There were goons in the building, probably behind closed doors for the most part, but no doubt others roamed the halls. They pounded on the walls and doors as I hurried along the ground floor hallway. So many infected. So many dead and returned, trapped in their homes and apartments, too stupid to rotate a knob or take a fire escape.

It was inconceivable, but no less true, and I hoped they continued raising a clamor. If the hunter heard them, he would think they had smelled him or one had seen him and set the others off with its moans. He would be nervous just knowing so many goons were nearby, and meanwhile their noise would mask my movements.

I passed the corpse of a little girl dressed in a blood-stained ballet outfit lying on her side in the downstairs hallway. She had been mostly dead for a long time. Her blond locks adhered to her face, caked with dried, blackened blood. When she looked up as I passed, the skin and hair peeled away from the side of her face, still stuck to the floor. She watched me, and slowly got up to follow.

I made it to the rear of the building in time to see the hunter through a window as he entered the back alley, gun raised, watching for the woman or a wandering goon. He focused on the street, as he should; so long as the doors to the alley were closed, there was little chance a goon would exit a building — unless the door opened by way of a push-bar rather than a rounded knob or lever.

I stood by the exit door and jiggled the round handle. From here, I couldn't see the man in the alley, but I was pretty sure he would have turned to focus his weapon on the door. I was careful to stand to one side of the doorway in case he shot through it. I listened. Footsteps on pavement. He was passing the door.

I jiggled the knob again, hoping he would think the woman he hunted was hiding in here, trembling as she held the handle. I hoped he would open the door and give me a chance to zap him.

But the little ballerina heard him out there, too. No doubt, she smelled him, like I did. She moaned, deep in her chest, and beat tiny hands against the door. I heard silence outside as the hunter stopped walking, but when the door failed to open — and with the moans from the other side telling him what was in here — he continued away from us.

I turned the knob. The little girl goon pushed the door open and stumbled into the alley. As she exited, I hurried back to the window. I doubted the man would waste a bullet on the child, not least of which because the gunfire, even muffled, could draw more goons. He would use a hammer or something to brain her, which meant he would lower his gun for a moment.

I watched the girl stumble in confusion. She saw the man off to her left, but she also smelled the blood spatter from the street to her right. She turned this way and that.

The rifle shifted into the hunter's left hand and dropped to his side as he grabbed a lug wrench from his belt and walked toward the girl. He raised his right arm to swing.

I fired through the window, catching him in the center of his chest. He fell back, and the little girl jumped on top of him. The building came alive with the din of goons, dead fists hammering on walls, doors, and floors. In the alley, the man struggled against the child as she clawed and snapped, getting teeth into his right forearm. He was still alive, but bleeding out fast. I think my bullet had cost him the use of his left arm, as it lay limp with the rifle still clutched in that hand.

He managed to shove the child back, tried to raise the wrench again as she turned and crawled toward him, but her teeth had severed the tendons in his forearm. He couldn't grip the handle, and the wrench clattered to the pavement. He kicked at her, snapping her neck back. Her head drooped at an unnatural angle, but she continued moaning and crawling toward him.

I stepped through the door, and dropped the girl with one shot. Now the man screamed, as much from sight of me as anything, I suppose. I must have looked like something out of a bad movie, dressed in the black suit with all the pads and belts, striding out of the death house with my guns drawn. He wasn't expecting to be the prey.

Frankly, he couldn't have anticipated something like me.

"Tell me what you see," I said.

He tried to make words, but nothing made sense.

I didn't take the chance of him raising his rifle. I

stepped on his left arm and kicked the gun out of his hand as he flailed in pain. Then I shot him in the head. He was too dangerous to keep alive.

I looked around for the woman he had been tracking, but I neither saw nor smelled any evidence she was nearby, possibly watching. Nothing else had come out of the alley or street yet, drawn by the gunfire, but overhead the block groaned its discontent.

I knew what they wanted. I had what they wanted, and I could barely keep myself from feasting right there. The smell of the huntsman's blood, even as it cooled, was exhilarating, maddening. The hunger screamed in my head, burned in my face.

My hands shook.

I holstered my pistols, grabbed the hunter by one leg and dragged him into the building I had just left. I went back out into the alley to gather his wrench and rifle. I left the dead girl where she fell. I was a little concerned about the trail of blood leading into the building, that it would draw too many goons, or worse: That other hunters were about in the city and would find the blood trail and catch me while I ate.

I locked the door's deadbolt and dragged the hunter down a hall away from any windows. I got some rain gear out of a pouch on my belt — a thin plastic poncho and plastic pants I had picked up at the sporting goods outlet — and I put them on over my outfit.

I stripped the body using the man's own hunting knife to remove his clothing. I gathered his weapons in a small pile, including the rifle, two grenades, and a pistol with a silencer on it. Then I set aside my gloves, cowl, glasses, and other gear.

And I ate. Started with his belly, burying my face in the softness of it and clamping my teeth, tearing flesh and muscle. His stomach burst open, acids draining, and the stench of it all made me tremble.

Oh, it was glorious and wild.

CHAPTER TWELVE: TERROR WEARS NO SHOES

Jane had no right to be alive. She told herself that when she awoke with a sudden intake of breath and sat upright in the little empty room with the shattered window and the bottom half of a dead creature turning ripe in the morning sun.

She had slept through the sunset and the dark of night, and nothing had disturbed her. Not the cold or the pain that ached in every bone and ounce of flesh. Not the noises from the street, nor the dreaded appearance of a clear-headed Z climbing the stairs in search of her. If that had happened, she wouldn't have awakened at all, she thought.

But as she sat in the morning light and massaged her bad knee, Jane wondered if that part had been a dream, if she had imagined the Z was more aware than his fellows, or if her panic had exaggerated a coincidental glance.

She flexed her left leg and grimaced at the pain. The knee was swollen and stiff, but the biker suit had absorbed much of the damage; she traced the scars on the leather and padded knee visible through her torn coverall. She took a Snickers bar from her backpack and ate it slowly, gently stretching her legs as she chewed. She risked a glance out the window, and verified that the mob had moved on, though several Zs remained trapped beneath the fallen pole, grasping at the air, scratching at the pavement.

On a good morning, she would go down there and knock holes in their heads. This was not a good morning.

Jane cinched her backpack tight, dropped George into her right hand, and limped to the door. She listened. She crouched and peered under the door, seeing nothing in the darkness beyond. She yanked the pen light out of her pocket and gripped it in her left hand, using her thumb and forefinger to turn the door knob.

The door opened only a narrow crack before she stopped it and listened to the darkness. After several quiet seconds, she switched on her light, revealing the dimensions of a second room, larger than the first, with two sets of frosted glass windows and other closed doors on each visible wall. A lobby of some sort, with offices arranged around it. Closed for decades, if the dust and lack of furnishings was any indication.

Jane eased into the room, scanned the walls and floor with her light. She checked the doors to the other offices to be sure they were shut, listened for sounds of movement within them. Nothing.

She continued to the doorway between the frosted panes. Again, Jane checked below it, this time spotting a ghostly illumination but no details, and nothing that indicated movement. She stood and listened. Opened the door a crack. Peered out.

Parts of a body lay scattered on the wooden floor, deflated flesh clinging to dry bones, the empty sockets of a ruined skull staring into her light. The corpse was alone on a landing where a staircase emptied onto the second floor of the building. Jane saw wooden hand rails leading downward, toward an indistinct light source. She hoped it was evidence of more intact frosted glass in the downstairs lobby, which would mean no Zs would spot her from the street.

She slipped out of the office, bypassed the dried remains, began descending the stairs.

Heard the sepulchral gasp of a revenant behind her as another office expelled its last occupant hard on her heels. Jane hadn't seen the open door ten feet away on an oblique angle, but the dead woman stumbling out of it had not failed to notice her.

Jane turned to meet the Z, set her feet as she readied George to strike. But her knee couldn't take the weight, and she fell sideways onto the stairs.

The woman lunged, broken fingernails and exposed bones clawing at the air between them. Her momentum rolled Jane backward, and they tumbled together down the stairs, bouncing at the bottom and rolling apart. The snack bags in Jane's backpack popped like balloons under the pressure, sounding like muffled gunshots in the open stairwell, and Jane's pen light clattered across the tile, light spinning against the walls as it traveled.

Jane shook her head. Her eyes wouldn't focus.

She heard the zombie woman scuffling on the floor and kicked herself away from the noise with her good leg.

Something grabbed her sneaker, and she kicked again, feeling a satisfying impact. She sat up, brought George down near her foot, and shattered a ceramic tile with a chime like a gong.

Her vision cleared, and she saw the Z plainly, a pale thing limned by the yellow light through oversized panes of rippled window glass fronting the lobby area. The Z had been an executive of some sort, dressed in a gray business skirt and what remained of a matching jacket. It wore a gold necklace. Dim light reflected from the word "dream" dancing over the dried apples of its exposed breasts as it pushed up from the floor and lunged at Jane again.

She stopped it with both feet, shoved it aside and rolled to straddle it as it fell. This time, George stuck true.

Jane spun, still squatting on the corpse. Nothing came out of the darkness or called from antechambers. No shadows moved against the windows in answer to their noisy struggle.

She tested her leg again, limped over to retrieve her penlight and zipped it back in a pocket. She went to the ornate front door and listened. Turned the deadbolts to unlock it. Cracked it open. Waited.

In her head, she pictured a map of downtown. Tried to visualize where the biker shop had been and how to make it back home by the most direct route.

She eased onto the sidewalk, closed the door behind her. The moans of the Zs trapped under the telephone pole carried on the still air around the corner. Jane put her back to the sound and limped as fast as she could bear in the opposite direction.

**

In Jane's absence, Maxwell took the day's watch. He sat in a lawn chair in the bed of the dump truck, his chin propped on a pillow resting on the rim of the bed, his eyes focused on the street beyond the junk wall. He wore a wide-brimmed hat to keep the sun off his head and shade his eyes.

For the first hour after sunrise, every time a cloud crossed the sky and shadows danced between the buildings, he caught his breath, hoping to spot Jane returning, yet fearing instead the sight of a lurching Z. It had been a long time since watch duty had triggered those fears, producing visions of zombie armies advancing on the junk wall and overwhelming the Compound. That never happened any more, not like in the first months. His imagination no longer ran away on him.

Not until Jane disappeared like she did, gone in search of her impossible cowboy. The gunslinger. The zombie killer.

Maxwell watched Willy, Johnny and Rita climb the fire escape on their way out into the city that morning. He nodded at the thumbs-up Willy offered just before the steel door shut. About fifteen minutes later, Maxwell again spotted the crew when they crossed to the north a few blocks away, and he realized his pulse was pounding; he took a deep breath and steadied himself.

If they ran into no trouble at all, it would take them a couple of hours to make the trip to gather the food and return. And he knew they would run into trouble somewhere. That's why he wished Jane was with them. They needed her out there. They always did.

The morning passed slowly. Maxwell ate a stale oatmeal bar. He drank a bottle of rain water. At noon, Moses appeared to give him a bathroom break. They didn't speak to each other, but Maxwell understood how much Moses wanted to yell at him for running off Jane. Maxwell jogged into the junkyard and went to the porta-john, then jogged back to his post in time to find the recon crew had already returned.

"Wait until you see the video," Rita said, raising a hand.

"Did you see Jane?" he asked.

"No, but we found —"

"Show me later," he answered. Then he told them to get into the Compound, get some rest, and he would join them when his shift ended.

Rita frowned, but Willy again offered a thumbs-up. Maxwell nodded at him and climbed into the truck bed, put binoculars to his eyes, dismissing the trio from his thoughts. In his peripheral vision, Maxwell could see Moses shaking his head before walking away. Maxwell was glad the others had made it back safe with more food, and he was gratified they had returned with something that appeared to support Jane's story about the gunslinger — at least, that was what they seemed to indicate — but he was still pissed off that she was gone.

He told himself he wouldn't stop making Jane squirm over every little slight until he heard an apology.

The day passed, and Xavier came to relieve Maxwell. The night passed, and Maxwell returned to the watch, sleepless and bleary, and only more confused by the video the crew had returned with the day before. By noon, he was parched, and pissed at himself, because he had forgotten to bring a water bottle.

When a human shape lurched around a corner three blocks away, Maxwell was too dry to gulp. He crouched low and used the binoculars. Focused in.

A woman leaned against the brick wall of a building, and for a moment he thought it might be Jane. But she was not Jane. Skeletal and naked, except for a windbreaker that flapped loosely on her emaciated body. Bruised and cut. Bleeding. She trembled and gasped for breath.

Maxwell wanted to cry out to her, to call for her to come this way to safety, but he didn't. He waited.

He couldn't encourage her to run his way if she was being pursued by Zs. She could lead a horde of dead to their doorstep. Better to let her die out there than to bring them here and be the death of everyone.

He crouched lower, ashamed but committed to the Compound's rules.

Maxwell watched the woman lean away from the building and look around, and now he could see that her eyes were blackened and swollen, desperation clearly drawn on her face. He also saw the moment of recognition when she spotted the junk wall and realized it was a zombie barrier, the sudden expression of hope so quickly replaced by the twinge of uncertainty.

The woman looked in all directions as if fearing a trap, then took a breath and shoved forward, stumbled, and fell face-first into the street. Maxwell heard the hard *smack* a second after she hit.

She reached both hands toward the distant barrier, the symbol of a border into a safer country, and sobbed.

She pushed up from the pavement, balanced on her hands and knees, teetering on all fours like a wounded doe. She wept and trembled, and fell over on her side.

Maxwell huffed and put down the binoculars.

He grabbed a blue signal flag from the rack by his perch and waved it so the Compound guard would see. Nancy was on duty again, he recalled; she signaled back with her blue flag. Nancy would alert the others that someone was approaching in the street, and Moses would scramble back out to the truck with a rifle.

Maxwell clambered off the truck bed and went to the junk wall, crouching beside a half-crushed Buick at the bottom of the pile. The roof rested on the backs of the bench seats, and the doors had bent outward at the top. Maxwell removed a rusty bolt holding a latch and opened the driver's side door. He crawled inside, gasping at the heat trapped in the hulk. In his silence, he heard the fallen woman cry out, and he wished he could see what was happening in the street.

He removed another bolt latching the passenger's door, gripped his hammer in his right hand, and opened the door, bracing himself for an attack.

Instead, he saw someone kneeling beside the fallen woman, and anger displaced his fear. He would not lose her now to some goddamn zombie!

Maxwell growled as he rose up out of the smashed car and started running, but he skidded to a halt when he recognized Jane at the woman's side.

"Jane?"

She glared up at him and jerked her head to one side. He looked at the hammer in his hand and put it back on his belt. Jane leaned closer to the woman and took one of her hands.

"It's okay," Jane said. "You're going to be okay. Are you bit?"

The woman's free hand fluttered around her head. She flailed and sobbed. Tears and snot mixed with blood and dirt on her face. She rubbed bony fingers across her cheeks.

"Please," she said. "Please, don't hurt me. Please don't hurt me."

Maxwell stood back from the woman, trusting Jane's read of the situation and giving them room. He looked at the junk wall to see Johnny and Rita waiting by the Buick. Moses stood on the bed of the dump truck with a rifle cradled in one arm, scrutinizing the scene with Maxwell's binoculars. He would watch their perimeter while they dealt with the mystery woman.

"Maxwell," Jane whispered.

He approached while Jane rolled the woman to check her body for bites or scratches.

"She passed out," Jane said.

"Are you okay? You look —"

He lost his voice for a moment as he saw the stranger's wounds up close, limbs and torso covered in bruises both fresh and faded, welts, and what looked like cigarette burns. Her wrists and ankles were chafed and raw, as if she had been tethered or chained — but no bites. Her hands, knees, elbows, and feet were scraped bloody from running and falling on concrete and asphalt. She stank of sweat and excrement, and she shivered when she breathed, like a child who had cried herself to sleep.

Maxwell wondered what terrible hell she had endured, how she escaped from it, and by what providence she traversed the dangers of the city to make it here.

"She's been tortured," Jane said, and Maxwell nodded.

He sighed and kneeled beside Jane as Johnny and Rita joined them. Rita put one hand to her mouth, but made no sound; mindfully silent in the wild. Johnny checked the woman's breathing and pulse.

"I eyeballed her for bites," Jane said. "She's clean. Well, you know what I mean. We need to move her inside."

Maxwell nodded, slid his arms under the woman, and effortlessly lifted her. Johnny went ahead of him back through the Buick and took hold of the woman under her arms to drag her to the other side. They were as gentle as they could be, and moving her was easier than they expected; she weighed nothing, really.

"Do you think she followed you back?" Maxwell asked Rita.

"No way. No body and no thing followed us that we didn't put down."

The chances of the woman stumbling across the Compound weren't that bad, Maxwell thought; all of the current group had arrived there by accident one or two at a time over passing the months. But the shape she was in made him worry that whoever had done this to her might be close on her trail. Might be out there right now, watching the group gathered around the truck. Might be planning an assault.

Once on the pavement inside the wall, they found the others waiting with a plastic litter Johnny had liberated from an ambulance months ago. They stretched their new burden out on it, and Willy and Johnny lifted the litter, starting back toward the junkyard.

Maxwell turned to Jane. He had noticed her limp, and she looked like hell, but he wasn't going to cut her slack. "You've got watch," he said.

"Bullshit. I found her, I'm staying with her. Anyway, if she wakes up, I'm thinking that she'd rather see women around than big guys like you."

He scowled at Jane. Then he nodded, asked Terrance and Moses to take the watch; Terrance was due to come on at sundown anyway, but Moses was supposed to cook that night.

"We need extra eyes on the lookout," Maxwell said, but Moses hesitated. His weren't the best eyes in the group, but Maxwell trusted him to make good decisions if they were confronted by the woman's pursuer.

"Keep a low profile and a sharp eye out. I'll join you soon, but I'm going to send Joey back out right away with a couple more of our guns. Just in case."

Rita told Terrance she'd bring him some coffee and dinner in a bit, and he reluctantly climbed into the truck bed. Moses waited.

"I'll bring you something, too," Rita said, smirking.

Moses smiled back at her and complied.

**

CHAPTER THIRTEEN: THE SHAPE OF TERROR

The men carried the litter into a mosquito tent erected above a wooden picnic table near the kitchen. They set the woman on the table just as Joey ran up with the First Aid kit from the supply house. Jane sent him back out for water — something for Jane to drink, something to share with the stranger, and some of the laundry water Jane could use to wash the woman's skin.

Johnny clucked his tongue and said, "There's really nothing we can do but try to make her comfortable."

Jane shooed the men away and Rita helped her strip off the woman's jacket, then roll her from side to side for a sponge bath. Brown water dribbled off of her and between the wooden table slats, pooling on the hard earth, slow to soak in. Jane used scissors from the First Aid kit to cut off the woman's tangled, crusted hair, then cloth-washed her head. She found two raised, discolored lumps on the woman's skull where she'd been hit hard recently.

Jane called to Joey: "Bring me a small jumpsuit and sneakers, some socks if we have them, and ask Polly and

Diane to come help us."

Joey hurried to comply. Polly and Diane arrived in seconds; the whole camp gathered nearby to learn about the newcomer, and the two women stood close enough to hear Jane call out. Polly, in her thirties, had been overweight before the end of the world, but she was now as wiry as the rest of the group. She retained a gentleness that most of the others had lost, though, and that's why Jane had wanted her help in case the newcomer awoke. Almost motherly, Polly represented the polar opposite of Diane: cold, cynical and suspicious, Diane wouldn't fall for any misdirection if the woman played on their sympathies.

Once they dressed the woman, Rita excused herself to go fill Moses' kitchen duties. Maxwell stuck his head into the tent and motioned Jane to join him, Johnny, and Willy outside. Maxwell had a video camera in one hand, and he stood beside Jane as he replayed the recording her scavenger crew had returned with while she was missing. They watched the images of Johnny and Willy examining the corpses on Market Avenue; the men didn't speak to each other, so the only sounds were their footsteps and echoes of wind. Johnny found the spot where the gunslinger had stood in the midst of the Zs, and he pantomimed firing at them, pointing at the way they spread around as they died for the final time.

"Most of them fell with what was left of their heads toward the buildings and their feet toward the middle of the street," Willy said from his seat on the ground. "Pretty obvious, someone had just walked among them and fired at close range as he moved."

The video changed angles, now looking down on the street from the height of the fire escape they had used to access the supplies in the apartment building. From this angle, the spread of the corpses became even clearer to the eye. The point of view suddenly changed again, now from the corner where Jane had hidden to watch the gunman, a slow pan across the street.

A final sequence showed Willy walking toward a Z as it closed on his position; they must have photographed this on their way back to the Compound, Jane thought. Willy had a meat cleaver in his left hand and a hammer in his right. As the Z shuffled within reach, Willy feinted left and the cleaver flickered with reflected sunlight. The Z looked left, following the motion, and Willy stepped to the right, slamming his hammer into the creature's head. It dropped, almost yanking him down with it before the hammer came loose from its skull.

"Amateurs. You're wasting battery shooting Z kills," Maxwell said and switched off the device.

"Is that all you have to say?" Jane demanded. "That video —"

"Evidently supports your story," Maxwell said. "We'll have to be on the watch for him again."

Jane waited for Maxwell to apologize for doubting her, but before she could enjoy the moment, Johnny spoke up.

"If he's out there, he'll come to us," Johnny said. At their curious looks, he added, "I found some spray paint in the building we looted, and I tagged the wall with our address so he could find us."

Maxwell drew his hammer and raised it, advancing on Johnny. He gritted his teeth and growled in frustration. He stomped the dry ground.

Johnny spun and came up on his feet, ready to fight. "What the hell, man?"

Jane stepped between them, barely able to keep from striking Johnny herself. "You fucking idiot! Do you see that woman in there? Tortured, starved, probably gang raped — you just told the people who did that to her where to find us, too!"

Johnny and Willy exchanged a look, hung their heads. Maxwell let out a deep breath.

"We'll need to go back and paint over that message first thing in the morning," Maxwell said. "Tonight, we'll set extra guards. With guns, I think."

Just then, Polly called to Jane. "She's stirring."

The woman whined, and all four of them moved toward the tent. Jane waved the men off and tried to quiet the woman.

"You're okay," Jane said, keeping her voice low. "You're safe. Nobody's going to hurt you now."

The woman's face twisted up, her cracked lips puckered, and she sobbed. No tears fell, though, and Jane knew that she was used up. Jane felt her chest tighten with a surge of compassion, then suppressed it by biting her own lip. No use getting attached to the stranger, she told herself. Not yet.

Jane offered the woman a sip from the water bottle, and she accepted it. The woman leaned on one elbow and tipped the bottle to her lips, spilling some on the jumpsuit. She patted the material gingerly, slowly realizing that she was clothed and clean. The woman stroked the skin on the back of her left hand with the fingers of her right hand, staring.

Jane wondered if the woman was more worried about the scratches and bruises, or amazed by her clean skin.

When the newcomer asked for more water, Jane motioned for her to drink. Then Jane spoke loud enough for Maxwell and Joey to hear her.

"Joey? Go get us a bowl of chicken soup. Have Rita thin it with water and warm it up. And bring another water bottle."

The woman nodded, whispered, "Thank you." She watched Joey run away through the mesh. She seemed shocked by the sight of a child. She eyed Maxwell, then looked Jane over.

"I promise you, no one will touch you," Jane said. "We're good people here."

The woman didn't look like she understood, and Jane wondered how long it had been since she was among "good" people.

"My name's Jane. That's Maxwell outside."

The woman took a breath. "I'm —"

She trembled with emotion, which caused her to cough. Jane didn't reach to steady her; she let the woman work it out for herself.

"My name was Lucy," she said. "They gave me another name, but I never forgot. My name — it's Lucy."

"You're safe now, Lucy. But we're kind of scared by your condition. Where you came from. How you were mistreated. We'd like to talk to you about —"

"Okay. I get it. I don't blame you." Lucy reached back to touch her hair, twisted the short bristles between her fingers. "I'll try."

Joey returned with a metal bowl charred black on the bottom. He passed it to Jane, who held it for Lucy as she sipped the thin broth. The woman moaned at the pleasure and relief of the food, and Jane's skin crawled. She sounded like the Zs when they fed, Jane thought. The sigh of death warmed over.

Jane took the bowl from Lucy. "Not too much too quickly," Jane said. "You don't want to make yourself sick."

Lucy thanked Jane for her kindness. She had another sip of water and took a deep breath. Looked at the people gathering outside the mesh. She sat up.

"The King of 32nd Street," Lucy said. "The Sun King. He's the boss-man. He makes the rules."

She sobbed again, shaking so that the water sloshed out of the bottle in her hands. Jane grabbed the bottle to steady it, avoiding contact with the woman. Lucy focused on Jane's hand on the bottle and took another trembling breath.

"Try to separate yourself from the events," Jane said. "This story didn't happen to you. It was someone else. They told you this story, and now you're going to try to tell us. To tell me."

"I'll try," Lucy said again.

"Think of it like a movie," Jane said, and Lucy's eyes widened. "The other person who told you this was a spy. She saw how many weapons the enemy had, where they holed up, how many soldiers, and she reported in to her superior. Can you do that?"

Lucy nodded.

"They live in a big brownstone off 32nd street," she said. "There's a fenced lot out back where they sometimes keep the biters for target practice. Maybe 15 men. Maybe more. I don't — the woman who told me this, she didn't know. Sometimes new men would show up, and new women would come into the harem room. Men would trade their women to be safe in the gang."

Jane looked at Maxwell, then the others. She saw in their faces how this information unsettled them. She tried to change the direction of the story.

"What weapons did they have?"

Lucy nodded again, focusing her eyes on a distant memory. "Rifles, machine guns or whatever. Pistols. Grenades. They wear uniforms. You know, stuff they raided from the surplus stores and National Guard blockades. Night vision — things. Goggles, I think is the word. Flame throwers. Knives. The woman, she heard them talking. She saw them. They got it all."

Jane let Lucy have some more soup, sip more water. Jane asked how the woman escaped.

"She didn't. She — I — One of the men was tired of shooting biters. No sport in it. He'd been saying it a while. 'No sport.' A couple of the women, though, they were mostly dead already. Wouldn't be missed. He was tired of them, too. 'Worn out,' he said. Said he'd give them a chance. Five minute head start at dawn. One of them didn't make it very far."

Maxwell spoke up, startling both Jane and Lucy. "Where is this man now?"

Lucy looked at the ground and seemed to shrink in on herself. Jane gave Maxwell a hand sign to be quiet.

"Lucy? How did the woman get away from the man?"

"I don't — I don't know. She heard gun shots, really close. And she fell down and waited to die. But when she didn't die, she got back up and ran some more."

Lucy looked at Jane. She reached out and grabbed Jane's forearm.

"Then she saw this place," Lucy said, and her face twitched as if trying to remember how to smile. "I — saw you."

**

CHAPTER FOURTEEN: MERCHANTS OF DISASTER

It was after dark when my senses returned, when the haze of blood madness passed, and I saw that I had made a mess of the hunter. Pieces of him littered the floor. Blood spatters smeared all around, even on the walls. It amazed me that I could eat with such wild abandon, and I wondered where the stuff went; I didn't have a working digestive system, and never excreted waste. So, did something new in me process the proteins and feed my brain? Was that thick black soup we seep when we bleed not actually coagulated blood at all, but somehow connected to how and why we hunger?

I doubted that I would ever know the answer, and yet I felt no disappointment at the prospect of remaining ignorant. I didn't need to understand how to construct a car engine in order to operate the vehicle, and I didn't need to understand the biology of the undead in order to feed my hunger. All I needed was a steady supply of food. And to ensure that, I had to gather a bit more information and locate a place to do my work undisturbed.

I stripped off the gory rain gear and suited up again, then left the building by the back door. A dozen goons looked up from the pavement when the door opened; they had been sniffing and licking the ground where the hunter had fallen, trying to draw sustenance from the blood trail. Two of them munched on parts of the little ballerina. When they saw me step outside, they lurched to their feet and started toward me.

I stood still, propping the door open, and I let them come. Five feet away, the closest one tilted his head to the side and changed course, veering past me to enter the building. He had smelled the fresh corpse inside. The others promptly followed him, even the ones that had been eating the little girl. I closed the door behind them, satisfied to hear it latch.

I decided to look into more of the buildings in the surrounding blocks. Warehouses, machine shops, and former sweat shops for the most part. I was in the old industrial district, a rust belt near the rail yard, where industry had shipped in and out of the city in better times. Many of the structures here had been abandoned as the economy tanked. This region became a haven for squatters. There could be a good place for me to use here.

The fourth building I checked had been a metalwork shop of some kind; the bottom floor had sliding metal doors leading to the street, a large work area with concrete floors and high ceilings. Rails with chains on pulleys evenly spaced overhead. Lathes and drill presses along one wall. Tool racks and work benches. Another sliding metal door led to a loading dock on an alley.

I liked this place. Off the trail the scavengers used, and a terrible area for them to search for food, it was unlikely that they would ever chance across it.

I found a number of goons as I traveled, and shot them down without trouble. One of them looked surprised as she fell, her eyes open wide and her bottom lip pouting, and I wondered if she had been awake and aware when I drew on her. Should have said something.

If more of us could think, and if we could overcome

our baser instincts of survival while avoiding killing each other, then we might be able to work together and overpower the food. Rule it. Farm it. I recalled an acquaintance in the old world who went on hunting trips during the winter. He would sit in camouflaged stands on someone's fenced wilderness property and shoot at passing deer. He called it "harvesting."

That's what my plan amounted to. Find the band of survivors, feed them, fatten them, and harvest them.

The night had ended by the time I finally headed back to Bob's apartment to gather my gear. I wouldn't need to sit and watch for the scavengers again, since I had the cameras in place. I could check them each morning before dawn — the humans were less likely to be about in the dark — and move them to new locations until I found the humans' sanctuary.

Rocky had returned to Bob's apartment building to wait for me, and when I approached, he trotted out to meet me. He still wouldn't get within arm's length. Instead, he circled around me, and as I watched him circle I noticed something I hadn't seen earlier: A message painted on the wall of the building the scavengers had visited. Sprayed on the bricks near the place I had stood when the peach-fuzz woman saw me shooting the goons. Their bodies seemed to radiate outward from the message.

The idiots wrote their address on the wall for me. After all the trouble I went to with the cameras, they sent me an engraved invitation.

I almost laughed. If breathing was still a natural reflex, then I believe I would have laughed. Odd as it was to recognize amusement, the emotion passed as suddenly as it had appeared, almost the very moment I became aware of it. I thought about the hunter and wondered if others of his tribe might see this message also. It wouldn't do to let rival predators find my food, not when I had just located them myself. Somehow, I would deal with the hunter's people when the time came, but meanwhile, I needed to protect my cattle from them — and from their own stupidity.

I saw the spray paint can they had used still sitting on the sidewalk, so I picked it up and sprayed over their message, obliterating it.

I knew where they hid. The junkyard southeast of here. All I had to do now was win their trust, prepare my new workroom, clear out any goons in the area, and watch for the hunter's people. It was doable. I was up to the task.

**

It took me better than three hours to walk to the interstate ramp where the discount warehouse stood deep and dark, front windows shattered, trash and dried corpses scattered all around. High noon meant nothing cast shadows in the lot. I moved slowly on my approach, not wishing to interest any goons in my actions. Rocky hunkered down in the tall, dry grass on the perimeter of the lot, content to watch.

The goons wandered aimlessly in the parking lot. Some sat, trapped, inside the cars where they had gone for protection before dying. Others seemed confused by the concept of a fence on the periphery of the lot. I didn't worry about putting them down. I entered the store through its garden shop, selected a wheelbarrow that rolled on two oversize tires, and pushed it into the store.

Now shadows were everywhere, and any one of them could be a human being waiting to kill me. I tested the air, but there was such a stench of decay here, of mildew and rotted meat, odd chemicals and other strange smells, that I couldn't pick out the aroma of fresh food.

I shoved the cart as far into the store as I could manage, trying not to make much noise. The place was a wreck. It had been looted, and it looked like a horde of goons had descended on the looters. Deep discounts, indeed. Display racks were upended, DVDs and kitchenware, clothing and toys broken on the floor. Corpses blocked the aisles, but they were all long dead, dried out, nothing that tweaked my hunger.

I went to the sporting goods department first, to see if any weapons remained. There were no guns or archery gear, but I found another decent hunting knife on the floor and put it in a belt pouch. A rain poncho in a small plastic bag still dangled on a peg hook, and I took it as well.

Then to the grocery department, walking on spilled macaroni and rice that had formed a gooey film in the water draining from the frozen foods aisle. I located some cases of Gatorade in a shopping cart and individual bottles of water in an aisle nearby. I had to step over bodies to carry the drinks back to the wheelbarrow.

The wheelbarrow had moved.

It was near the spot where I left it, but it faced in another direction. Someone had been here, checking to see what I might have found and left in the cart. They must have followed me in; if they already lived in here, then they already would have secured the store's edibles. They must have been disappointed to find my wheelbarrow empty, I thought, and they would be waiting close by to steal what I put in it, possibly even to kill me for it.

I pretended not to notice, kept my head down, and carefully placed the drinks in the cart. I turned and walked back in the direction of the grocery department. Rounded a corner and paused. Listened.

Light steps and the rustle of plastic. Someone rooted in the wheelbarrow.

I drew two pistols and stepped around the corner, leveling them in that direction.

"You don't want me to shoot," I said.

The man with his arms full of Gatorade bottles froze in place, bent over the wheelbarrow. I couldn't see him clearly in the dim light of this vast steel cave, but I could tell when he looked up at me.

His voice was a hoarse whisper: "You shoot, and those zombies outside will rush in here."

"Yes. But I could get out of here … while they're tearing you apart."

I stepped closer. My face burned with hunger, and I gritted my teeth to keep from moaning. I was going to eat this man, of that no doubt existed in my squirming brain, but I didn't want to share him with all those goons outside. I had to be smart. I took another step, wondering if he was alone or if someone hidden even now drew a bead on me.

A haggard strip of a man. Wild hair and an unruly beard. Clearly, he was hungry too, I thought, as I watched him glancing around at the shadows.

"There's enough for us all to share here," the man said. "No reason to fight."

Us all? I thought, and knew for sure that he was not alone.

"Who else is here? Better show yourself. Or I shoot him now."

"Ain't nobody else," the man said, carefully placing the drinks back in the wheelbarrow. "Just me. By myself. You let me put this back —"

I shot him. Aimed for the kneecap, but hit him in the thigh. It was a quiet *pop*, using the silenced pistol I had picked up from the hunter yesterday, but it worried me that something outside might have heard. To his credit, the man shoved his hand in his mouth and stifled his own scream.

But the shot did bring another shape out of the shadows, a woman who rushed to the man's side and looked at me with desperate eyes. She was not as rail-thin as the man; she still had some meat on her bones, which meant he had been taking care of her better than himself.

I was close enough now to see her fear. Close enough to smell it on her. It was like Thanksgiving came early.

My left hand trembled as I holstered my second pistol and reached in a pouch for a roll of duct tape. She might have noticed the trembling, but she couldn't have known it was not fear or a rush of adrenaline that made me shake. It was desire. I could barely contain myself. The man's blood was driving me insane, and the rounded flesh moving across her bones —

I tossed the roll of tape at her. I preferred to use tape rather than handcuffs, though I had a set of those as well; tape was easier to handle.

"Wrap his wound tight. Do it fast, before the goons smell it."

She grabbed the roll and whipped it around her man's thigh, pulling it taut to stop the bleeding.

"Now his wrists," I said.

She hesitated, looking from me to him and back again. I shook the pistol at her to urge her to hurry, and she did as she was told.

"Now, wrap your own wrists."

She tried, but couldn't make it work. She only managed to tangle the tape around both wrists. I stepped forward and put the pistol to her head. Slick with tears, her face reflected moonlight as she cringed and sniffled, and her man shook with rage and pain beside her.

"Get on the floor. Face down. Hands behind your back."

"Don't you hurt her," the man hissed.

I didn't plan to hurt her. Yet. I planned to make her push the wheel barrow — later, after I finished eating her boyfriend.

I wrapped her wrists together, then her ankles. I stretched tape over her mouth, around her head, and over her eyes. I did the same to her boyfriend, then I popped him with the stun gun. While he was dazed, I dragged her through the store, shoved her in one of the frozen food cases, stunned her, too, for good measure, and closed the door. I didn't tell her to chill, though I thought about it.

I went back and found her man. Dragged him into the front section of the store, into a restroom, and I started setting my gear aside. I put on the poncho I had just found.

He stirred when I cut the duct tape off his thigh, and he thrashed when I bit down on the bullet wound. Blood gushed into my face and down my throat, hot and coppery, and supercharged with fear. He soon grew quiet, and I feasted, lost again in the ecstasy of the flesh.

**

Hours later, I finished loading all the bottles of water, Gatorade, canned food, and so forth that I thought the wheelbarrow could handle. I helped Bobbie, as I had decided to call her, to climb out of the rotted food in the cooler, and cut her ankles loose so she could walk over to the area where more Gatorade bottled littered the floor. I opened a bottle and cut the tape away from her lips so she could drink. I held the bottle to her mouth and poured. She choked and spit. I let her have some more.

I whispered to her that she should not talk. No questions. No screaming. Goons lurked just outside, and she did not want what they would give her.

"You stink like rotted vegetables," I told her. "That should keep the goons from scenting you."

She nodded. I got out the handcuffs I had lifted from a policeman's corpse and cuffed her to the wheelbarrow. She didn't complain. She didn't ask about her boyfriend; if she had any sense at all, then she knew he was dead. She didn't ask why I smelled so bad or wore safety glasses in the dark store. She resigned herself to whatever fate I had in mind for her, and I suspected she thought I would want to keep her alive for sex, if not for companionship like her boyfriend had done.

She was at least half-right.

"You two got in here past the goons somehow," I said. "Show me."

She nodded and shoved the heavy wheelbarrow through the dark aisles. She struggled with it at first, but soon got used to the distribution of weight; I kicked things out of her way when we came to blockages — fallen shelves, crushed Styrofoam coolers, corpses. She led me into the stockroom, where giant boxes of unopened treasures still stood neatly stacked in rows. On this side toilet paper, tampons, shampoo. On the other, yarn, silk flowers, greeting cards. I grabbed a couple of packs of the toilet paper and a box of maxi pads, and added them to the wheelbarrow, thinking that might make some of the humans as happy as seeing all the food and drink I would leave for them.

A happy hog doesn't watch out for the knife.

Behind the building was a loading dock. One roll-up door was wide open, and I wondered why survivors hadn't come here to strip the place clean in the early days of the plague. Then again, the mess in the main store probably meant they had tried, only to meet their match in goons.

Bobbie pushed the wheelbarrow down a concrete incline, past parked semi-trucks and an industrial Dumpster. Nothing moved in the back lot. She pointed to a break in the chain link fence around the pavement, and I held the fencing aside far enough that she could push her cart through. Beyond was a dry retention pond with wide concrete culverts leading into the depression. We followed one of the ditches around the outside to the front parking lot, moving slowly, quietly on the barrow's big wheels. Rocky joined us, coming close enough to sniff Bobbie's leg.

I noticed when a goon in the lot spotted us and turned to watch us pass. I glanced at Bobbie and recognized the terror in her eyes; she saw him too. He didn't moan or try to attack. Our shuffling gait, combined with the smell coming off my corpse, must have kept him from thinking we were food. But he raised his face to look in the direction we walked, perhaps considering the probability we were on the scent of something edible. He shuffled in that direction.

Flocking behavior, I thought. I needed to put a stop to that before others joined him. I didn't need a herd following me back to my kitchen.

I touched Bobbie's arm and she halted. She knew we were being tracked, and she kneeled between the handles of the cart, trying to disappear. I left her there, walked over to the fence line, and the goon in the lot changed direction to investigate us.

I wondered which of my tools would work best, and chose the hunting knife I had just picked up in the store. When the goon leaned against the fence to peer at me, I stabbed him through the left eye. He stared at me with his remaining one for a full second without a sound, then dropped to the pavement, the skin of his face peeling off along the chain link as he fell.

Bobbie had tears in her eyes when I reached for her. She stood slowly, trembling, staring at me in the night.

I knew that should have made me feel sad, or something.

**

CHAPTER FIFTEEN: FORTRESS OF SOLITUDE

Dead zombies rotted in the heat. Where decay had been slow to touch them before the gunslinger put holes in their heads, gasses now fully engorged them, plumped them like sausages on a barbecue, ready to burst. Clouds of flies circled them, laying eggs, filling the street with the loud hum of their wings.

Jane and the rest of her scavenger team smelled the dead before they reached the block, and they heard the buzz of the flies before they caught sight of the corpses. They stood in the street and stared at the dead as insects made meals and birthing suites of the remains.

On the wall beyond the carnage, squiggles of spray paint obscured the message Willy and Johnny had left behind. The junkyard's address was illegible.

Jane signaled the group to retreat, and they jogged back along their trail to a place where they could bear to breathe without gagging.

"You think your gunman covered up the address?" Johnny asked Jane.

She nodded, although she wanted to argue that the gunman wasn't *hers*.

The others agreed. "Maybe he knows about the gang on 32nd Street," Rita said. "Or at least he's aware there are bad people out here."

"That pre-supposes that he's a good-guy," Johnny said.

Jane stepped back. She hadn't considered that the shooter might be a danger to them. He killed Zs, right? What's not to like?

"So, what do we do now?" Willy asked.

"I say we circle to the other side of the building, go up and grab more supplies," Johnny said. "Maybe he'll come back while we're here."

Nods all around carried the consensus. Despite her limp, Jane led the way, stopping when they had mounted half of the fire escape. She massaged her leg through the layers of coverall and bike suit. She wished the others wore outfits like hers, but Maxwell had declared the bike shop off-mission, not to mention in an area thick with Zs. He wouldn't allow another excursion there unless circumstances changed.

Jane looked out over the portion of the city she could see from this vantage, listening for any Zs, watching for any shadows in alleys that might conceal a hunter's movement. She hated that moment in movies when someone would comment on the quiet, and someone else would answer, "Too quiet," but this appeared to be one of those moments.

She thumped herself in the head for talking to herself, even if she did it silently.

"Something?" Johnny asked, looking up at her.

"No, nothing," she whispered.

"It's too qui—"

"Don't. Say. That."

Working in teams of two, the group soon cleared two more of the apartment floors, stacking food by the fire escape and checking the street as often as they could. As the day's work wound down, Jane took a moment to rest and stared out the hallway window. She wondered how the masked gunman might alter their survival chances. She worried about the rape gang from which Lucy had escaped; if they knew survivors were hoarding supplies here, they would come in and take the food, and if they knew where the survivors were hiding out, they would overrun the junkyard, rape and eat the people, and save the canned goods for later.

Jane hoped Johnny was right, and the gunman had painted over their address on the wall — but she also hoped that Johnny was wrong about the danger the gunman posed to the Compound. She didn't like to admit it, but the image of him mowing down Zs had given her something to hang onto.

"Jane!"

She whirled toward the harsh whisper, crouching, ready for a fight. George was a familiar weight in her right hand.

Rita stood in the doorway of the last apartment on the floor, one she and Johnny had started to clear. She waved for Jane to join them inside.

Jane signaled, *What?*

"You're going to want to see," Rita said.

Jane relaxed, let George dangle. She slid past Rita, who stayed behind to watch the exits, and entered a living room. Bookshelves covered the walls, loaded to overflowing with books of every color and size. A telescope on a tripod stood close to the main window facing the street. Empty food cans and boxes scattered on the floor. The place stank of human waste and old paper.

"Johnny?" Jane said, trying not to speak too loudly.

"In here," came his soft reply.

She passed through the living room, down a short hallway, past a door marked with a chalk X — probably a bedroom or guest bathroom; she had memorized the layouts of these apartments, and they only differed when they contained additional bedrooms. Johnny hovered in a doorway at the end of the hall, and he motioned for her to hurry.

She looked into the room. More bookshelves lined the walls, but what amazed her was the evidence of how the resident had survived after his food ran out.

He lay naked in his bed, attached to an empty bag of I.V. fluids hanging from a pole. He was emaciated, his skin a pasty yellow in the dim lighting, and Jane thought he probably looked much older than he was. The sheets were filthy with his urine and feces. Fat black flies buzzed in the room. More empty I.V. bags lay strewn all around the bed, and books had been dropped on them as the man read to himself in his last days.

He had the foresight to raid a hospital, she thought, or perhaps to bring home supplies when he abandoned his post at a hospital, but he had lacked the courage to raid his neighbors' apartments.

"He's not dead," Johnny said. "Yet."

Jane gasped. She hadn't seen the man draw a breath, but even as Johnny spoke, the man's chest fluttered. His lungs rattled.

"Is this safe?" she asked.

Johnny shrugged. "I'm going to see if there are any more medical supplies we can take."

Jane nodded and stepped closer to the dying man as Johnny rummaged around the bedroom. On instinct, she studied his skin for signs of a bite, but in that way at least, he was clean. She lifted the front of her jumpsuit to cover her nose and filter the man's stench as she leaned closer to him.

His eyes opened, and she thought she'd jump out of her skin for a moment. She realized George was in her hand only when it clanked against the I.V. pole.

The man's breath caught in his throat. His Adam's apple bobbed.

"Don't eat me," he whispered.

"We won't hurt you," Jane said. "We thought everyone here was dead."

"Close enough."

Jane crouched beside the bed, trying to understand what she was seeing. "Why?" she asked, unable to find the words to be more specific.

He understood her, nonetheless. He seemed to smile with his eyes, though no other muscles on his face responded until he spoke.

"I read. I'm no hero. This is no world for me. But I'm too much a coward to kill myself."

"We'll take you with us," Jane said, and she saw Johnny pause and glare at her.

The man shook, and Jane realized he was laughing.

"Listen," he said. "I've seen things. Do you know about the camo men? The bad guys?"

"Yes. They hunt people."

"Not surprised. Watch out for them."

Jane nodded, leaned closer.

"Have you seen the man in black?" the dying man whispered. "The one who kills zombies?"

"Yes. We're looking for him."

The man's eyes closed. He seemed to grow smaller, like a beach inflatable losing pressure. Jane waited. She saw his chest flutter. His eyes opened.

"What about smart zombies?" he asked.

Jane gulped.

"He's oxygen deprived," Johnny said. "He isn't making sense."

Jane shushed Johnny, and whispered to the dying man. "Some of them," she said, "they can think, can't they?"

Johnny came up beside Jane and touched her shoulder. "What was that?" he asked.

Jane glanced up. "Some of the Zs can think. They're smart. He's seen them. I think I did too."

"One of you is delusional," Johnny said, returning to his task.

Jane sat back on her heels. The man seemed clear-headed enough just a moment before, but he had stopped breathing for several seconds. Maybe he was in some kind of near dream-state, she wondered. Maybe both of them were.

"What's in his I.V.?" she asked.

Johnny answered without turning around. "It's a basic saline solution. He was trying to stay hydrated. Looks like he had run out of the good drugs. You'd think he'd have saved some morphine or Dilaudid for the end."

Jane watched the man struggle for another breath. She asked him his name. Suddenly, that was the most important question in her mind. She didn't want to call him "I.V. Guy" any time she thought about him in the days to come.

His eyes cracked open, and he looked at her. Breath moved between his lips, and then it didn't, but his eyes never closed.

Jane collected several of his books to take back to the compound, and some of them had book plates inside the cover. Each of the plates were inscribed with a different name.

**

CHAPTER SIXTEEN: THE TALKING DEVIL

Early on the morning after Bobbie and I arrived at my warehouse lair, I walked along the surrounding block to find an area where a large number of goons stumbled randomly in a close bunch. I was just about ready to start luring the humans out of their junkyard, but too many goons still lurked around and might try to take my food if they got the chance. I needed to continue thinning the mob before I began my mission.

Besides, Bobbie would still last a few days.

Rocky stayed clear of the crowd, watching me as I matched their gait and shuffled among them, unnoticed. I bumped shoulders with them. The throng shifted, seemed to find a common direction and moved together like a flock of birds — wheeling, settling on a wire, then rushing back into the air because one of them got spooked.

I raised two pistols to the heads of two nearby goons, one to either side of me. Fired. The pistols were silenced, but the simultaneous barks and falling victims brought every head around, and the crowd surged toward me. I immediately lowered my arms and merged with the movement of the mob, as if I too were looking for the source of the racket. They pressed against me, pushed past me. A few fell upon the corpses of the goons I had just shot. One of them pulled at my clothes, but turned away when he smelled me.

This was a dangerous game. At some point, it stood to reason, one or more of the dead would attack me before figuring out that I wasn't food. I imagined them ripping into my flesh, tearing off my limbs. A feeding frenzy could erupt, and I would be taken apart before they realized I wasn't their favorite flavor.

It was not the ending I was working toward, but I couldn't say that I feared such a thing. If it happened, then it happened. But if I was going to increase my own prospects for feeding, then I had to get the population of hungry goons under control. It was a chance I had to take.

Survival instinct apparently can continue to function without fear as a driving force. I learned more about my new existence every day.

Having found no obvious food, the crowd began to disperse once more, and I picked out two more heads to shoot. I fired, lowered the guns, and moved with the crowd again. Someone grabbed my shoulder, and I pulled away. That was usually enough to dissuade the casual goon, but the hand grabbed my shoulder again.

I turned toward it, raising my pistol.

"No! No!" croaked the dead man who had pulled at me, holding up his hands to ward off my weapons.

I hesitated, watching the other zombies as they rounded on this new figure speaking in their midst. One snatched at the dead man's shirt, mouth wide to bite, and I shot it in the skull.

Now the crowd turned toward me, but the dead man's continued flinching and gasping beside me immediately grabbed their attention. He started to speak again; I could see his mouth trying to form words. He was over-thinking the process of drawing in air and making sounds now, after having reacted initially without analyzing how it worked.

I watched him struggle, trying to determine if he was experiencing fear. I put the flat side of a pistol against his ashen lips and caught his eyes. He stayed quiet.

We stood still like that for several seconds as the horde studied us, sniffed us, prodded us with cold fingers. One by one, they lost interest. I waved him after me, and he followed as I led him along the street and up onto the sidewalk, away from the cluster of goons. Rocky dropped back, keeping his distance from the new stranger.

We paused together in an alleyway, and I looked around to make sure there were no dead people walking close by. Rocky crouched and watched us.

"You just woke up," I said.

He nodded and spoke in hideous gasps of air. "Heard you … shooting. You shot … someone right … beside me."

I looked him over. His body was in much worse condition than mine. He had either been dead longer than I had been, or he'd been in some serious scrapes. Pieces of arm meat dangled through torn shirt sleeves. His mangled bare feet, covered in sores, seeped black mucous with each step. His thin brown hair was gapped and falling out, though that might have started long before he died. He had the look of a banker or an accountant, with beady eyes and twiddling fingers.

"You just woke up," I repeated, as much for myself as to help him focus.

"I don't know … how I got here."

"You followed the mob, followed the food."

"You're like me. … You're dead. … I can smell it."

"Yes."

"But you're killing …"

"Yes. Killing zombies." I holstered one gun, kept the other between us. "Too many dead, too little food."

He looked out on the street, watched the crowd

down the block as its members wandered aimlessly. I raised the gun behind his head and almost pulled the trigger. Then I thought about how useful it could be to have some help with my scheme, and I wondered if there soon would be more like us. Maybe my condition would prove to be more common than I initially believed. I lowered the pistol.

"Why not … just shoot me?" he said, turning back to face me.

I holstered the second pistol. "I have a plan."

I led the man to a sporting goods store four blocks away. I had been there before, and I knew what I was looking for. It was a slow slog, but we weren't in any hurry. I asked his name, but he couldn't recall it. I told him to call me Dan.

"Is that your name?" he asked.

It was not, but that was what he could call me. I didn't answer him, regardless.

"I'll call you Bob … until you remember yours," I said.

"What's in a name?" he asked, and I saw his gray face clench up as if he had felt a pain. He blinked — something else the dead don't do, but that I hadn't realized until that moment. He had forced himself to grimace, forced himself to blink. Maybe he was experimenting with his muscles, attempting to remember what it was like to be alive. Maybe he was remembering the time he died.

"It's like … dreaming you woke up," he said. "Then really waking. But falling back asleep … before you get up … and then dreaming you got up."

I just looked at him. I had no idea what he meant.

"I keep waking up, or dreaming I'm waking," he said.

I got Bob some socks and a wetsuit of similar design to mine, some golf gloves and tinted ski goggles. While we shopped, I outlined my plan to him. I found a roll of athletic tape and used it to seal his arm hole and wrap his feet before getting him into the new zombie-fighting uniform. We pilfered the hunting and camping area for useful items, including more gas bottles for my torch, flashlight batteries for a pair of Maglites, and so forth. No guns remained in the store, but I found ammunition for the pistols I already had collected.

"Why not just … shoot me?" he asked again.

I didn't answer this time. It was a reasonable question. May even have been a request. But until he stopped asking it, there was no way I was giving him one of my guns. If he wasn't suicidal and he thought I might end him, then he was sure to try to end me.

"Talking will get easier … as you practice," I said. "Everything gets easier. The suit is to protect you from more damage … and to hide your condition from the food. The goons won't mess with you if you move slowly … mimic their direction of movement … and above all, do not talk."

We continued along the street to a shoe store and found some boots he could wear over his scuba booties. Bob chose a fedora on a rack of hats by the cash register and perched it atop his diving suit headpiece, and I realized I would not have liked him in the old world.

I reconsidered shooting him.

"I'm hungry," he said.

I nodded and waved for him to follow me.

"You always will be," I said.

**

Bobbie was awake when we arrived at the warehouse. Pale and pasty, her naked body shimmered under a sheen of cold sweat. Her arms and legs were extended and bound to opposite ends of the oak work table I had dragged to the center of the wide space. Bleached yellow hair with brown roots plastered to her face. Eyes red, rimmed in shadow. Tiny veins across her face had ruptured when I fed earlier, and she had tried to scream into the duct tape I wrapped around her head. She again tried to scream at the sight of us, but the cry came out as a hoarse whine, and her face turned red as the morning sun.

I closed the heavy sliding door, threw the latch that sealed it against accidental entry, and led Bob over to the table. I didn't mention to him that I had been calling the woman Bobbie. He was smarter than your average goon, after all, and I thought that might make my long-term expectations for him a little too obvious.

I stroked the hair out of the woman's eyes. I *shushed* her. She trembled, and silent tears cleared streaks through the dirt on her face.

Bob held back a pace. He felt the eternal hunger, but I had warned him not to attack her or I would shoot him. This was a delicate operation. And it was a learning experience for all of us.

"I found her two nights back," I said. "She was with a man, hiking through the city … looking for food … on their way somewhere else. Who cares. They found me instead. I killed and ate the man, and made her push a wheelbarrow loaded with supplies. She's stronger than she looks."

I showed Bob my tools on the nearby work bench. Saws, hatchets, hedge clippers, bolt cutters, torches. Even a cleaver, carving knife, and butcher's block.

I pointed out the fresh burn where the woman's left breast had been. The skin puckered and bubbled. The wound seeped.

"We keep her alive as long as we can so the food lasts," I said. "We take only what we need … and prevent her from bleeding to death. We don't bite her directly … so she doesn't get the plague and turn. She'll still get infections … most likely … but she won't live long enough for that to do her in."

Bobbie whined. She tried to cry, but the pressure of the tape on her mouth just forced bubbles from her nose. She choked, panicked at the lack of air. I wiped her nose with a piece of oily cloth and told her to blow. Blood came out when she blew.

Bob stepped closer. "I'm so hungry," he said.

"I know."

"I had been hungry all the years … my noon had come to dine…"

He was quoting someone. I almost recognized it. But more importantly, he was waiting for me to allow him to eat. Like a dog balancing a treat on its nose until the master whistles, he was willing to play by my rules. So far, so good.

I picked up the carving knife in my right hand and took hold of the woman's remaining breast in my left.

"Deep breath," I said to her. "This is going to sting."

**

CHAPTER SEVENTEEN: CARGO UNKNOWN

Maxwell came awake ready for a fight, and reached for his hammer. It wasn't where he had placed it when he went to sleep. A couple of seconds ticked by as he shook his head and got his bearings. He saw Willy standing over him, clutching the hammer, and realized Willy had carefully moved the hammer away from Maxwell's hand before nudging him gently with the toe of his boot.

From the look on Willy's face, Maxwell knew the man was unsurprised by his reaction. He always awoke ready to fight.

Willy handed Maxwell the hammer and said, "We were leaving for another scavenge run, but there was something in the street. You need to see this."

Maxwell wiped his free hand across his eyes. He motioned Willy toward the door and pushed himself off his bunk. "Where's Jane?"

"She's on the fire escape, watching the street until we get back."

"What is it? What did you find?"

Willy waited for him outside the bus door, and Maxwell closed the door and latched it as he exited. He never left doors standing open. Ever.

"A stack of food cans and boxes, water bottles. Gatorade, Max — Gatorade!"

"Just sitting in the street?"

"There was a walkie-talkie on top, and a notebook. We didn't touch any of it. We wanted you to see it first."

Reasoning that someone might be watching them, and not wishing to give away their front line bolt-hole, Maxwell followed Willy up the fire escape, through the building and out onto the opposite fire escape, where Jane waited with Rita and Johnny. Nobody said anything. They followed Maxwell down the steps, but he looked up and ordered Jane back onto the top landing to keep watch.

She was still on his shit list for hogging the cereal and then nearly getting herself killed, and it was important to him that everyone saw her obey. She didn't argue.

"My knee hurts anyway," she said.

As he approached the mound of supplies, Maxwell found himself counting the boxes, categorizing them, thinking about the empty spots they would fill in the pantry. This was a good haul and would feed them for several days, maybe a few weeks if they were careful.

"Do you think it's booby-trapped?" Willy asked.

Maxwell shook his head. That wouldn't make sense. Why would an enemy destroy all this food just to take out a couple of men? He reached for the walkie-talkie on top of the notebook and read a note taped to it:

"Turn this on at high noon only. Channel 19."

Under the walkie-talkie was a spiral bound notebook with "Read Me" scrawled in Sharpie on the yellow cover. Maxwell set the radio aside and opened the notebook. The handwriting in it was rough, as if it had been jotted down by someone with arthritis. But it was legible. He read aloud:

"Don't leave the safe zone you've set up. Goons

aren't the only bad guys out here, so keep your eyes open. I'll bring food and supplies again when I can. If you need specific items, leave me a list here. Put it in a jar or something that won't blow away.

"You have more questions than I can answer right now. This is what you need to understand: My uniform is coated with something the eggheads invented that repels the goons. It allows me to walk among them for short periods and keeps them from following my scent. It also stinks like rotten garbage, but I'm getting used to it.

"I'm not alone out here, and we're working to clear as many goons as possible from this area so we can begin leading you to the safe haven at Sunrise Shore. I will give you details when I can.

"Switch on the walkie-talkie only at high noon. Channel 19. I will try to be in a safe area and contact you at that time. Save the batteries.

"Dan."

Maxwell glanced at the others. "Let's get this stuff back inside. Then we'll gather up, and I'll read this to everyone."

He looked up at Jane. She was going to be one self-righteous bitch now. Not that he deserved any different. He waved at her. She waved back. He would not have thought body language could clearly say, "I told you so," if he hadn't seen it for himself.

It took two trips from each of them to get the goods upstairs. That was a lot of food, Maxwell thought. If only one guy had carried all this here and left it for them, then he must have used a wheel barrow. Something with big wheels that didn't make a lot of noise.

This "Dan" guy had managed to stay out of sight of their lookouts as well, so he must have come in the middle the night, after the moon had set, and approached from an angle that kept the building between them. He knew right where to go so that they would spot the goods when he was ready for them to see them, and not a moment sooner.

That meant he had been watching them for a while.

"I don't understand," Moses asked after Maxwell read the note to the group. "Why didn't he just announce himself?"

"Maybe he doesn't want to have to answer a lot of questions," Nancy offered.

"More likely, he wants to be sure we don't jump him and take his zombie-proof suit," Maxwell said. "He's playing it safe. He knows we're here, but he doesn't know for sure if we're good guys or not. Maybe he's had run-ins with the Sun King, or one of the rape gangs, or some of his people have. I'm betting he'll never set foot in the Compound, and he'll high-tail it if we try to intercept him."

"We could, you know. Take the suit, I mean," said Johnny.

None of the group responded, though their faces spoke volumes. Maxwell realized some of them were wondering if that was such a bad idea. He was pretty sure a couple were imagining wearing the suit and running for the countryside.

"I know we only have a few rules, but I'd like to believe that's not how we operate," Maxwell said, standing to walk around the circle of survivors. He focused on Lucy when he spoke again: "We look out for each other, here. We feed each other and protect each other. And when someone offers to help us, we don't betray him."

She didn't look convinced.

Then Maxwell turned to Johnny. "When the time comes that it's safe to leave, we will not turn on the ones who come to help us."

Johnny's cheeks flushed. He stared at his hands as if looking for something he had lost.

"No harm done, man," Maxwell said, clapping the younger man on his shoulder. "We all thought it."

Johnny nodded.

Moses looked at the sky. "It's about ten, ten-thirty."

Jane finally spoke. "I've been looking at this walkie-talkie. It's not designed for long-range use. With the buildings around here, he'd be lucky to get a signal to us. Unless he's in one of the buildings. Or on top of it."

Maxwell nodded. "Take some binoculars. Just before noon, get to the roof of the Ashmore and see if you can spot him."

The Ashmore was the tallest building in their safe zone. Still, it was only ten stories. She wouldn't see to the roof of the taller buildings outside the zone, and she'd only be able to spot the mystery man if he stood in the open. Trying to eyeball him would also mean that she'd miss hearing his transmission. Jane wasn't sure it was a fair trade.

"I want to hear what he has to say," she said. "Besides, I've already seen the man."

"I'll go," Johnny said, and Maxwell wondered if Johnny was hoping to make up for suggesting that they ambush Dan — or if he was thinking he might spot Dan and go after him alone.

**

Everyone but Johnny gathered around Maxwell as the sun hit its zenith. Jane led Lucy, who was still wary of the others, to sit close to Maxwell. The tension was palpable, but it was a good thing for once. Each person in the group seemed to feel like they'd reached a turning point.

All but Lucy, who touched Jane's hand and whispered to her.

"Something's not right," Lucy said. "I heard Sunrise Shore was overrun. One of the King's men, he talked about it. He said he had to shoot everyone in his group to distract the biters so he could escape."

Jane caught Maxwell's eye; he had heard Lucy too. Sunrise Shore was an island resort a mile off the mainland, connected by a divided four-lane bridge. At least a two-day walk from this part of the city. It made sense as a safe zone, easily fortified, if it was free of infected people. But was it?

Maxwell took a breath and switched on the walkie-talkie. It hissed, and before he could send a signal out, a voice came over the speaker:

"You there? Anyone?"

Maxwell squeezed the button and answered. His hands shook, and despite his misgivings, he broke into a grin like no one had seen in a long time. Everyone in the group smiled, and a few laughed like hyenas. Even Lucy caught the bug for a moment. Jane hugged Joey and leaned closer to listen.

"We're here, Dan. My name is Maxwell."

The voice that answered him sounded tired. "How many with you, Maxwell?"

"Twenty-eight souls. How do you plan to get us to the island?"

There was a pause, and Maxwell thought he might have failed to transmit. Then Dan answered: "One at a time, at first. I'm hoping they can make … more of these suits."

"Amen to that," Moses said, and the others mumbled agreement.

Maxwell shushed them. "Dan, we had heard Sunrise Shore was overrun."

"Just like everywhere else, Max, but we managed … to clear them out. Now listen, I can't move you yet," Dan said. "There's some thick infestation ... between here and there, and a few … rogue gangs. Just sit tight."

"We can do that. Thanks for the food, and the other stuff."

Again, several seconds passed before Dan responded. Maxwell almost called out to him, but the radio crackled and the voice returned.

"Anything else you need?"

Maxwell looked around the group. They needed just one thing, and Dan had already supplied that. He had given them hope again. A reason to hang on. Maxwell could see it in the faces that surrounded him.

"No, Dan. We're good. You take care of yourself out there. We've also heard there are some bad guys on 32nd Street that are armed and — well, evil sons of bitches."

"We're aware. We'll be careful. I'll check in again in … 48 hours if I can. If I miss that check-in, then I'll try again the next day. Spare the batteries. Signing off."

"Over and out."

Maxwell felt the hands grabbing him, the arms enfolding him as he switched off the walkie-talkie. Everyone was hugging, and no one was having flashbacks of the clutching hordes.

Polly, who had been there longest of all, sobbed silently, and Lucy put a brittle hand on her shoulder. There were no shouts of joy, no hallelujahs. Just quiet embraces, back slaps. Rita and Moses kissed. Joey jumped into Jane's arms, and she spun him in circles.

Maxwell looked at them all and felt warm inside. "You know what, people? I say we splurge tonight and have a hot meal. I'm cooking."

"We should all get cleaned up and wear something nice if we have it," Rita said.

"And somebody go fetch Johnny," Maxwell said.

Jane went, but Johnny was nowhere to be found.

**

CHAPTER EIGHTEEN: THE SPOTTED MEN

Just before noon, I was on a rooftop two blocks away from the humans' encampment, preparing to make the call. Bob was a block further away, hidden behind a boarded up window near the top of an office building, watching to see if the survivors sent someone out of their haven to track me down.

Bob spotted a man in gray coveralls when he climbed to a rooftop in their safe zone and began scanning other buildings for sight of me. Bob watched the man walk around his rooftop, pausing and focusing his binoculars. Bob could also see me, crouched in a rooftop gable where no one from the encampment would be able to spy me, not even Johnny.

I learned all this when Bob picked up his walkie-talkie, set to channel 23, then sent two tones through to the second walkie-talkie I was carrying. I picked it up and asked him, "Anyone there?"

It was a question any listener might expect to hear, and if the humans were scanning other channels rather than saving the batteries like I told them to, they would think I was calling out to them on a different channel.

Bob sent back one tone for "Yes," which would mean nothing to anyone else who might be listening.

"Any movement out there?"

He sent back two tones. *No*. Which meant the person looking for me was not moving from his position.

"Is there danger?" I asked, which Bob understood was to determine if I was in danger, not him.

Two tones. I was okay for now.

"Switching," I said.

One tone. He was ready.

I picked up the first walkie-talkie, which was set to Channel 19, and turned the power nob. The speaker hissed. I pressed the "send" button and called out to the humans, but they didn't answer. I waited. I called out again, and this time they responded. We talked.

About the same time that Maxwell asked me when I could begin moving the first of them to safety, Bob transmitted three tones.

I responded to Maxwell, and while he was talking, I picked up the other walkie-talkie and asked Bob what was up.

"Man on the move, headed my way," he said, abandoning all pretense of coded language. "He's armed."

I needed to get off the damn "phone." I stood up and walked to the edge of the rooftop, chancing a look at the street. I could see a young man in a jumpsuit climbing down the fire escape of a building on the edge of the junkyard's safe zone. He must have turned to face Bob's building and seen something there, a reflection off of Bob's binoculars perhaps.

I finished talking to Maxwell and headed down my own set of stairs; I moved slower than the look-out did, and I had farther to travel to get to the street. I called Bob on the way down, told him to head for the roof of his building and then take the fire escape down on the far side. We had prepared for the eventuality that someone would come looking for me, but I hadn't expected them to spot Bob. We would have to improvise — a talent for which, generally speaking, dead people aren't well known.

By the time I got to the street, there was no one in sight. I kept to the alley that would shield me from view if anyone else took the man's place on the lookout for me. He was inside Bob's building by now, headed up the stairs or possibly the fire escape on the side of the building away from me. The few goons in the building might distract him or even end this in our favor, but I knew I couldn't rely on them.

You can't trust a goon.

I circled, saw Bob slowly descending the metal stairs on the far side from the human compound. He raised a hand to let me know he saw me too.

I had to decide what to do. I got out one of my pistols and tried sighting at Bob, just for practice. I could not aim that well from this distance; my hands were not steady enough or nimble, and there was no way I'd be able to shoot this human if he started down the fire escape.

Zombies work best from up close. I knew this, but I would have to try a long distance solution anyway.

I motioned for Bob to hurry down, and even as I did, I spotted the man moving past the windows of a tenth floor room. He was about three floors higher than Bob now, and if he came out onto the fire escape, he'd catch Bob in no time. Our scheme would be blown. I had to divert the man somehow.

I looked at my pistol again. I had a silencer for it, which I retrieved from a belt pouch and screwed onto the barrel. I circled to the south side of the building and started firing into a window on the eleventh floor. The sound of breaking glass would bring the human to investigate, I hoped, and he might not realize he'd been suckered until it was too late for him to catch up to Bob.

I circled back again, careful to keep out of sight of anyone looking out from the building, and fired into some windows on the twelfth floor this time. A big piece of plate glass fell, and even Bob noticed. The goons trapped inside the building moaned and banged on the walls. I tried to will them to intercept the human in their midst, but they persisted in being useless.

Bob hurried as best he could, and we were together on the sidewalk when the man finally saw us and searched out a fire escape landing.

He yelled at us once, perhaps thinking that we could dispatch any goons attracted by his voice. We ignored him and headed west. We knew he would follow.

"I saw him notice me. I stepped back from the window, but it was too late," Bob said.

I grunted. There was nothing else to say.

A block over, we cut north into an alley. A wandering goon watched us for a second, then followed. We could hear the man's shouts grow closer. I sent Bob ahead to the next corner, while I crouched beside a Dumpster with my gun drawn.

The goon looked at me, then fell in behind Bob, who hesitated just long enough that the man spotted him turning the far corner. He also saw the goon in pursuit of Bob and slowed his run, trying to decide what to do. The man jogged past me, and I fired the pistol again.

I missed.

The bullet hit the bricks on the other side of the alley, and he looked over there; the noise of the shot itself was muffled enough that the *SMACK* of brick and bullet was much louder. He stumbled.

I heard the goon moan and knew it was turning toward the man. He pointed a pistol at it, but I fired again, hitting him in the buttocks, and he fell to the pavement with a shout. His gun clacked and spun on the pavement.

I hurried to him. He clutched at his bleeder and thrashed on the ground. He bit his lip to keep from screaming. Then he looked up at me.

"Why did you shoot?" he asked.

I got out the stun gun and stuck it to his chest just as the goon made it to us. Bob came back around the corner in time to see me shoot the goon in the head. Then I shocked the man again.

I made him breakdance.

Bob had his duct tape out when he reached us, and he quickly wrapped the man's wrists and ankles, as well as his bleeder.

"Because you could not stop for Death … we kindly stopped for thee," Bob said.

Bob put the man's pistol in his belt. He hooked his right hand under the guy's left armpit, and I took the right one. This kid was heavy. He was solid and strong.

He would last a while.

**

CHAPTER NINETEEN: THE STONE MAN

Maxwell built a fire in a steel drum and put a screen across it. The Compound didn't have fresh meat, but they had liberated some cans of corned beef hash and cans of Thick'n'Hearty soup, so Maxwell warmed those in a pot. Joey passed out Gatorades to everyone and they toasted each other. They toasted Dan, their savior, and they toasted Johnny, wherever he was.

Johnny had made his choice, like all of them had the right to do. Others had left before him. All those who remained behind could do was wish them safe journeys.

But Jane fumed that Johnny failed to return before dark. It was irresponsible. She suddenly understood why Maxwell fussed when she was late returning to camp, but told herself this was different. She could take care of herself; she had no such confidence in Johnny's ability.

The others believed Johnny had gone after Dan, and some feared he might have killed Dan for his zombie-proof uniform. Maxwell wouldn't allow anyone to search for them, preferring to follow Dan's request to remain safely in the Compound.

They each had a possibility in mind, a favorite version of Johnny's fate. Maybe Johnny ran into Zs. Maybe he caught up to Dan, surprised him, took his safe-suit, and bugged out for parts unknown, leaving them to fend for themselves. Or possibly Dan killed Johnny in a fight over the suit.

Jane had no preference. She saw Johnny's fate like the cat in Schrodinger's experiment, a favorite subject of one of her classmates not that long ago. Vastly simplified, the thought experiment supposed that a cat in a sealed container could be both alive and dead simultaneously until observation confirmed one state or the other. It was an absurd supposition, she thought, and that was Schrodinger's point: Mathematics may allow for either state, or both simultaneously, but real life allows for only one.

There was no simultaneously contradictory state of existence. You couldn't be both alive and dead.

Until now, Jane realized. What were the Zs, if not both alive and dead? Whether they were observed or not. Any time she was scavenging, she could open a door and find a dead body or open a door and be attacked by a dead body. Chew on that, Mr. Schrodinger.

Maybe Johnny was like the Zs. He was both alive and dead until observation of him collapsed all his possibilities to a singular point. Until he was observed, Jane supposed, then she would just imagine that Johnny was both alive and dead. That made him more or less like most of the other people in the world right now.

She corrected herself: While Johnny was both alive and dead in her current cosmology, all those others out there in the wild were neither dead nor alive. She took another drink and laughed at herself.

Physics was hard.

**

Jane sat on a ratty folding chair and ate her soup,

watching the others celebrate for the first time since the world ended. They didn't try to be quiet, but neither were they particularly loud; this level of noise would be dangerous in the wild zones, she thought, but here in the depths of their Compound, with the comfort of knowing Dan hunted the Zs outside, a little party probably would not be the death of them.

Moses wore a white dinner jacket and black tie, no shirt. Rita had a long red dress and heels, making her tower over Moses even more than usual. They swayed together as if dancing to a favorite song; Jane wondered what they were humming.

Maxwell was in his usual dingy black jeans and T-shirt, with his hammer in a holster. A faded plastic rose was pinned on his shoulder.

Each of them had sought some way to join in the spirit of the celebration. Jane had changed into a fresh jumpsuit, opened a pack of neon pink laces and relaced her sneakers. A plastic Daisy poised behind her ear.

But Lucy, still dressed in the simple jumpsuit Jane had given her, sat off to the side of the group and watched the buildings surrounding the compound. The flames from the drum caused gigantic shadows to flutter and dance against the deeper shadows of the structures. Jane noticed Lucy and wondered what it would take to make the woman feel safe again. She knew Lucy expected this dream to end badly; Lucy still could not believe she had escaped her own special circle of hell and might be graduating from this relative purgatory to a real sanctuary soon.

"Okay, everybody," Maxwell said as he finished his hot meal. He held up a blue plastic coffee container and shook it, an oversized rattle.

"I gathered some stones in the lot this evening," he said. "Twenty-seven whitish pebbles, and one black one. We'll each reach into the jug, and the one who draws the black stone will be the first to travel with Dan to the island."

Jane pointed at the jug. "Take out a white stone."

The question on Maxwell's face was clear, so Jane explained: "Johnny."

He nodded, removed a stone, and tossed it into the yard.

"Shouldn't we send women and children — or in our case, child — shouldn't they go with Dan first?" asked Moses.

Maxwell looked at Joey, then Lucy, then the rest of the group. "I didn't think of us that way. I thought all of us deserved an equal chance."

He shook the jug again, and waited.

Moses glanced around the circle, saw the resolve in everyone's faces, and nodded. He motioned for Maxwell to continue, and he said, "Who wants to pick first?"

Joey's hands went up. "Me!"

Jane grabbed the boy under his armpits and stood him in the middle of the picnic table. Maxwell returned their grins and held the jug high over Joey's head, so the boy had to stretch to reach inside it.

Joey drew out a white stone, plumped out a pouting lip.

"Draw one for me," Moses said.

Joey drew a black stone. People gasped, including Moses, who looked at Rita. Jane saw the tears in her eyes, and wondered if Rita was overjoyed or heartbroken.

Moses shook his head. "Maxwell, take a white stone out and put the black one back in. I'm not leaving until Rita does."

Maxwell didn't argue. He took a white stone out of the jug, put the black one back in. He looked around the group, reached in, and withdrew another white stone.

"I'm not leaving until you are all safe," he said.

There were rumblings that the game was no longer being played fair; Jane and Willy both said so, but Maxwell just shook the container again. This time, he walked through the group, letting each person draw their own stones. White came up over and over. Lucy drew white, and Willy, and Nancy, and Rita. Everyone drew white.

Finally, it was Jane's turn.

"We all know what's left in there," she said when Maxwell held the jug out for her. "I want Joey to draw it."

Maxwell looked at the others. They didn't object. He held out the jug so Joey could easily reach inside, and Joey just peeled back the plastic lid, put his hand inside, and brought it back out again. Pinched between his forefinger and thumb was the black stone.

No one hesitated. Everyone cheered as if the reveal was a surprise, then immediately put their hands over their mouths and bent low.

The cheer echoed among the buildings, bouncing this way and that, finally returning to them from another direction, sounding ghostly.

Jane picked up Joey in her arms and hugged him.

"Now we need to get you packed for a trip," she said.

**

On the second day after Dan first spoke to them, at high noon, Maxwell switched on the walkie-talkie and called out. After a few seconds, he called again. In the silence that followed, Maxwell saw the anxious faces of his people, the terror that hope would abandon them so easily. He called once more.

"I'm here, Max," said a tired voice over the radio.

"We were concerned," Maxwell replied.

"I almost didn't answer you," Dan said. "One of your people … came after me. Attacked me."

"Are you okay?"

"I will survive."

Maxwell hated to ask in front of the others, but he had to: "What about Johnny?"

Silence.

He repeated the question.

"I heard you," Dan said. "I never got his name. Our fight drew goons. Your man didn't make it."

Maxwell heard gasps. He looked at the others. Jane was stone-faced. Tears ran on Nancy's cheeks. Joey buried his face in Jane's arm.

"Dan, we're very sorry. Johnny was not supposed to do that. To go after you."

"Max, I'll be clear. There are other groups I can help first. I don't need your kind of trouble. I won't be back in contact. Do you understand?"

"Please, Dan," Maxwell said, his big hands shaking. "Please don't abandon us. We have women and a child that need you."

The walkie-talkie did not respond.

"Dan, please! Don't leave us here to die. Dan?"

Silence.

Maxwell rubbed his palm against his eyes and paced.

"Dan, if you're still listening, please, please call us back tomorrow," Maxwell said. "We'll check in each day. Please don't damn us for Johnny's sin. I'm begging you. I'm begging."

If Dan was listening, he gave no sign.

**

CHAPTER TWENTY: THEY DIED TWICE

As I climbed down from my rooftop vantage, I left the walkie-talkie turned on and listened to the man, Maxwell, plead for mercy. The desperation in his voice made me hungry.

Bob met me on the street. If he could have smiled, I believe he would have.

"He sounded frustrated," Bob said. "The end of every man's desire."

I didn't ask him what he meant by the quotation, because I sensed he wanted me to ask. He felt superior to me because he could recall bits of poetry he had read during his life.

He was deluded.

"We'll let them stew," I said. "They'll be more willing … to play strictly by our rules, when we return to help them."

"I've been thinking about that," Bob said. "When they see us, we need to look like heroes."

I stopped walking and stared at him. He turned.

"I'm thinking of cowboy hats," he said. "Dusters.

Our silhouettes should be … cinematic."

Deluded or not, he was right. I knew there was a reason I kept him around.

"I know just the place," I said, changing course for a Western-wear shop in the garment district.

**

Johnny's skin was pale, and his limbless torso stuck to the work table, caked in dry blood. His eyes fluttered open with the clatter of the steel door, and I watched his face as he struggled to understand what he saw.

We were dressed like post-holocaust cowboys now, wide-brimmed Stetsons and long leather coats. I traded my safety glasses for reflective aviator sunglasses with wide leather side-shields. They reduced my peripheral vision, but honestly it wasn't that great without them.

For a few seconds, Johnny's face tried to smile around the duct tape that kept him quiet. I imagined he was deciding if he had lost his mind or if help had arrived. Then terror widened his eyes and he trembled, a reaction that set his stumps flopping on the tabletop like the fins of a wounded walrus.

I grabbed the dirty syringe from the work bench and gave him a hit of morphine. His eyes rolled back, but not before I caught the look of gratitude in them.

"Life is sweet, but after life is death," Bob said.

Johnny would last us another day. The hunger was quelled for the moment; if not, then neither Bob nor I could have withstood the aroma of blood that soaked the wood and concrete. And I knew others would catch the scent as well, if we didn't consistently obscure it.

I pointed at a white bottle on a shelf, and Bob took it outside to pour bleach around the building and confuse any goons that happened along.

We were ready, at last. Things would begin happening fast tomorrow. We would need to go over our plan tonight.

And then, we would eat.

**

In the junkyard, nothing seemed to be happening fast. Time had stopped. Maxwell ordered everyone to inventory their supplies and prepare themselves for a long wait, but he also forbade Jane and the rest of the scavenger team from leaving the camp.

Jane finished checking her gear and personal bug-out kit, then retreated to the mosquito tent and cracked open a *Gideon Argo* novel; the scavengers had brought back lots of books over the past few months, like those Jane had taken from the I.V. Guy's apartment, but Jane quickly discovered she no longer enjoyed reading anything except pulp fiction and adventure. She kept returning to the yellowed paperbacks that had belonged to the original tenant here, the man who first let survivors inside the gate after the waves of death had washed over the city.

He had a sizable collection of *Doc Savage* and *Destroyer* novels, as well as *Playboy* magazines. Jane wasn't interested in the nudie-mags, but she was drawn to the pulp stories from a naive time when men and boys believed they could overcome any threat with a combination of brains and brawn. The lurid titles, like *The Jade Ogre* or *The Running Skeletons,* seemed to fit her own time too well. She'd seen her share of both in the real world, but reading about them metaphorically was different somehow, transforming these adolescent power fantasies into her own stories of triumph. Argo was like a modern Savage, though, and she liked the alliteration in his adventures – "Castle in the Clouds, City in the Sea" – not to mention the name of his support squadron, "The Flying Zombies."

Jane looked up from the book, *Gideon Argo and The Lost Lemurians*, when Moses opened the door and entered the nearby pantry building. She returned to reading, but the door opened again, immediately, and Moses backed out of the pantry. He closed the door and sat on the stoop. He propped his elbows on his knees and put his head in his hands.

Jane set aside the book and walked over to the pantry.

"You okay?" she asked.

Moses shook his head. He looked up at her, his eyes brimming with tears.

"Thought I was past being sad," he said. "Thought I couldn't feel like this no more."

A rock formed in Jane's throat and dropped like ice into her bowels. She stepped around Moses and opened the door. Morning sun lit the pantry, the shelves crammed with cans, bottles, and boxes. Wood floor, exposed rafters.

And Rita, hanging by her neck from an orange electrical cord tied to a rafter, a step-stool tumbled on its side below her pointed toes. Her face was purple, her tongue swollen out of her mouth, her eyes distended. She was dressed in her regular work coveralls, which she'd soiled as she died.

"God damn it," Jane said.

Jane exhaled between clenched teeth, then righted the stool, climbed high enough to reach the cord with her hunting knife, and cut Rita down. The woman folded up as she hit the floor, her ligaments popping. The little building shook.

Jane left Rita's corpse lying in a heap and joined Moses on the stoop.

"Wait here. I'll go get Maxwell," she said. "Don't let anyone else go inside."

Moses nodded.

Jane headed for the gate, where she found Maxwell talking with Nancy. She interrupted.

"I need you to come help me with Rita," Jane said, and before Maxwell could ask, she continued: "Moses just found her hanging in the pantry. I cut her down."

"God damn it," Maxwell said, and Jane nodded.

Moses had not moved when they returned, but he wasn't alone. Joey had joined him, sitting on the stoop with an arm around the older man.

"Joey, go get one of the burial blankets," Maxwell

said.

Joey nodded and ran off.

Maxwell touched Moses on his shoulder, then went into the pantry. Jane followed him and closed the door. The room felt small to her now.

"If Dan hadn't abandoned us," Maxwell said, kneeling beside Rita.

"If Johnny hadn't been a reckless shit," Jane countered.

Maxwell nodded. This was not Dan's fault, and Rita wasn't the first of them to take this escape route. If she were, they might have felt something more.

"Guess it's good you dug those holes," Maxwell said.

Joey called from outside, and Jane cracked the door to accept the blanket; it was musty and damp, one of a pile they had set aside as good for nothing else but shrouding the dead. She handed it to Maxwell, who stretched it out and rolled Rita onto it. He wrapped it tight, then lifted the bundle over his shoulder.

"Need a hand?" Jane asked.

"I got this."

Maxwell walked away through the junkyard, and Joey asked Jane if that was Rita in the blanket. She said it was.

"That's too bad," he said. "She was nice."

Jane nodded. Rita was nice. She was also gone now, and Jane wondered how long it would be before she had trouble recalling Rita's name.

"Run get me some wash water," she said. "I need to clean the floor in here before people start coming for lunch."

Joey ran off again, veering past Lucy, who had settled under the mosquito tent with Jane's paperback. She didn't look up.

Moses stood. His eyes were dry.

"Thanks for helping," he said.

"No problem. I think she would have done the same for me."

Moses blinked. He looked like he was confused.

"I don't think you would ever do that," he said. "Rita, now, she had talked about it a few times. Dan gave her hope, and then he took it away again."

"That was Johnny's fault," Jane said.

"Does it matter?"

Moses stared off in the direction Maxwell had gone. He shrugged in answer to his own question, put his hands in his pockets, and followed after Maxwell.

Of course it didn't matter, Jane thought. Least of all to Rita.

**

CHAPTER TWENTY-ONE: THE FRIGHTENED FISH

I sat on a rooftop, walkie-talkie to my ear, and listened to the man, Maxwell, plead for "Dan" to answer. It was like watching a float bobbing on a fishing line, waiting for the little red plastic bubble to sink, and timing your pull for the moment after the fish takes the bait.

On his fourth try, I told him I could hear him.

"Thank God," Maxwell said. "You didn't abandon us."

"I have orders to get you all out. That's the only reason we're talking."

"I wish your orders came through yesterday."

"What does that mean?"

"One of our people killed herself."

A cold pinprick tickled between my eyes, the closest I came to having an emotional reaction. The thought of wasted food almost upset me. No moaning over spilled blood, though. Decided I didn't care, but I told Maxwell I was sorry about that. He didn't respond immediately.

After a few seconds, he said, "Just tell me what you need from us."

"Dawn tomorrow. You'll see me two blocks away from your wall. Send one person out. No weapons, no gear. We will handle that. When we get him to safety, we'll contact you and arrange another."

"You have back-up?"

"I do now, after what Johnny tried."

"Dan, we have a child here. We would like to send him out first."

"How old? Can it keep up with us?"

"He's ten or eleven. He'll manage."

Again, I let him wait for my answer. Let him stew while I imagined what we might do with a child, how long it could survive, or if it had better uses than as a quick snack. I considered that a child was a good test of our plan; if we could successfully fool the child, then we would be better prepared when they sent us a full-grown man. And, he could also be used to test another question I had, about how bites cause the change and whether a bite from me or Bob would make a human into a smart zombie.

"Fine," I told him. "Send the boy out at dawn. No tricks this time, or you're on your own. And stay in your compound. No more trips out for supplies. We'll drop some off."

"Okay. We understand."

"Send the kid out to us alone. Wait one hour before you come out to get the supplies. Then get back to safety. Any attempt to intercept us will be … answered with extreme prejudice."

"We understand."

"And Maxwell, give the kid a bandana or something … to cover his mouth and nose. These uniforms reek."

**

The next morning, Jane stood on the ladder to the fire escape, waiting for Joey to say his goodbyes. There had been no party last night, no celebration of their impending liberation. Rita's death cast a shadow over the group. But as Joey made ready to leave, everyone met him at the inner gate for a last hug, or handshake, or wave before turning him over to Maxwell, who walked him to the building where Jane waited.

"Why not use the bolt-hole?" Joey said. "It would be faster."

"The bolt-holes are secret," Maxwell said. "We only use them for emergencies."

Joey nodded. "I just hate to climb stairs."

Maxwell looked up at the building and thought, *Me too, kid.*

"Jane will see you off," Maxwell said. Then he kneeled and gave the kid a hug. "You listen to Dan. Do as he says. Be quiet, be brave, and keep moving. If shit gets real, what do you do?"

"Climb."

Maxwell nodded and motioned toward the fire escape. Jane picked up Joey and set him on the ladder, patting his butt to start him up the rungs. Maxwell walked to the dump truck and hauled himself up onto the roof, then used Rita's binoculars to scan the street for signs of Dan or his men.

The sun, a dim red glow behind the buildings, cast shadows on this side of the glow that were deep and impenetrable.

Jane and Joey paused at the top floor entrance, and while Jane opened the door and looked into the corridor, Joey waved at the people below; he couldn't see them down in the dark, but he knew they were there. Maxwell wondered about the wave. Nobody waved anymore. Was hope of reunion a prerequisite for a goodbye wave?

Jane took Joey's hand and drew him behind her into the building, closing the door behind them.

Maxwell once again watched the street. He thought about what Jane was telling Joey right now; they had talked about it in the night. She would step out onto the fire escape on the far side the building, close the door, and sit by Joey while they waited for Dan to appear.

"I know you're scared," she would say. "You'd be stupid if you aren't, and you're not stupid. Just remember the rules."

And Maxwell knew Joey would recite the rules back to Jane: "Be quiet. Watch your six. Know your exit. And if shit gets real, climb."

Jane would probably tousle Joey's hair or give him a hug, Maxwell thought. She would tell him he was smart and brave. She would give him the face mask with elastic cords they had taken from the First Aid kit so he wouldn't complain about Dan's smell. And then, when the day had brightened enough to see Dan standing two blocks off beside a pile of cans, boxes, and bottles, she would send Joey down the fire escape by himself.

When Maxwell saw a figure materialize out of the alley shadows, his heart pounded. His right hand went to his belt to grasp his hammer. His left hand shook, and he lost focus. He forced himself to steady, to see, to be ready.

The man in the shadow wore a Stetson and a brown duster over a black body suit. Bandoliers crossed his chest, and a leather work belt held bulging pouches, no doubt stuffed with tools, ammunition, and rations. The man had pistols in both hands and some sort of dark glasses on his eyes. His nose and mouth were covered by his black suit's head gear. He was tall and imposing. A true gunslinger. A goddamn hero.

No wonder Jane had been so sure of what she saw that day, Maxwell thought. He let go of his hammer and raised his right hand to signal greetings.

Dan, or whichever of his backup crew this might be, raised his right hand also, waving the pistol slowly to be sure Maxwell understood his meaning. Then he slid the hand inside his duster and holstered the gun. He kept the other pistol ready.

Several minutes passed before Maxwell saw Joey's silhouette in the street, approaching Dan. Dan raised his right hand out flat, motioning for Joey to stop; muffled voices carried along the sepulchral street to Maxwell as they spoke to each other, like whispers in a graveyard.

Joey turned to wave up at Jane, who was still waiting at the peak of the fire escape. He waved at Maxwell, who waved back; an unaccustomed response, and it made Maxwell feel uneasy. Then Joey cut in front of Dan, entering the shadow of the alleyway. Dan gave a last jaunty salute at Jane, then followed Joey into the dark.

Maxwell let go of the breath he had been holding. He waited for Jane to return, but she did not. Willy and Xavier climbed up to join her, however, and at the appointed time, they gathered the supplies Dan's crew provided. A case of bottled water, boxes of breakfast cereal, toilet paper, cans of beans.

Maxwell reached up to help Jane down from the fire escape, but she waved him off. She didn't speak. She looked at him with eyes as red as the sunrise, and limped to the bus.

"You'll see him again soon," Maxwell said.

Four days later, Dan answered the noon call on Maxwell's walkie-talkie: "I hear you, Maxwell. We can pick up another traveler. Send one out at dawn tomorrow."

"Is Joey okay?"

"He is. He sent you a note. I'll leave it with some more supplies in the morning. Are you all well? Need anything?"

"We're good."

"Glad to hear it. Stay put, follow the directions, and we'll get all of you … soon enough."

**

CHAPTER TWENTY-TWO: THE THREE DEVILS

The man they sent out to us was called Xavier. In his forties, he would have had a bit of a paunch if he hadn't gone hungry for so long. Wiry build and feral eyes. I didn't like him. He looked stringy. He would be tough eating.

"Hey, guys," he said as he reached the street corner where I waited. The black bandana tied across his mouth and nose bounced in the low light of breaking dawn, and he kept his voice low out of habit, not wishing to draw goons.

I gave him a wave to follow me, and started north. After a long look at the new guy, Rocky heeled. Xavier paused at the corner, looking at Bob, who hung back at the dark end of alley, out of sight of the humans.

Bob motioned for Xavier to fall in step. "I'll bring up the rear," Bob growled.

Xavier nodded and began trailing me. He hooked his thumbs in his belt and picked up his pace, but I held a hand up to stop him.

"Keep a little distance," I said. "Give me a few yards

of lead to watch ahead … and leave some distance between you and Bob."

Xavier nodded.

"And don't talk unless you see goons," Bob added.

Xavier didn't mention the stench. Must have heard the talks I'd had with Maxwell. They expected the smell now. Good. Less to explain.

I paused at the next corner and raised one finger as I turned west. Wiggled the finger to indicate that Xavier should follow me. Heard him gasp when he reached the corner and saw me walking up to a goon in the alley.

It was a tall man, a head higher than me, with biceps that showed he was a gym nut in his lifetime; in a fair fight, he would have taken me for sure. But he didn't even notice me.

I was dead to him.

The goon angled around me, pale eyes locked on Xavier, a moan rising like a drowning man's gurgle from deep in his throat. I let him pass, then whirled on him and took off his head with my machete. The body crumpled to the ground, and the head rolled nearly to Xavier's feet. The face was turned toward the pavement, but we could see the mouth still trying to work, causing the head to wobble.

Xavier stomped it under his combat boot, splashing black goo.

I gave him a thumbs-up and continued westerly.

We turned north again, made another block, and I saw a shadow move in a doorway near where we would make our next turn. A woman stood up. She wore a tattered dress that had once been bright with yellows and reds, a flower print, but was now a uniform shade of dirt. She'd had long blond hair, but hunks of it were missing, leaving bald patches on her skull. Her skin was the same shade as her dress, but seemed to be intact.

Even from this far away, I could tell she was dead. Unlike the goons, though, which moved like sleep walkers, she had the inhuman movement of a puppet pulling her own strings, having to think about how her muscles were supposed to work. There was a consciousness to her motion that neither goons nor living persons exhibited. Neither of them had to think much about walking or grasping or biting, as it was just something they did. She had to think, though.

She was aware.

I came to a halt, motioning Xavier and Bob to wait. I looked back, seeing how Xavier was studying the woman and trying to gauge Bob's stance, trying to decide if either of them had realized what was going on. Bob slid his pistol into a holster and put his hand on the stun gun in his belt. He was ready if we had to subdue Xavier. I turned back to face the woman and started forward again.

For several seconds, she stood still and watched me approach. Her face angled to regard each of us in turn with her pale eyes. Then she withdrew into the shadow of the doorway. She seemed as frightened as she was curious, and I wondered how her emotional development compared to mine or Bob's.

"What's going on?" Xavier said. "She's acting strange."

I shushed him, motioned him to wait. Bob closed within reach of the man as I approached the dead woman. Xavier gave Bob a glance, wrinkled his nose, and covered it with the neck of his shirt.

"I died for beauty … but was scarce adjusted … in the tomb," Bob said.

I looked back to see Xavier glancing sidelong at Bob. It wouldn't do to let him study us too closely, nor should I keep the lady waiting. One thing at a time.

I spoke to the dead woman in hushed tones so Xavier would not hear. "You know what you are?"

She gasped, drew air into her lungs and expelled it in a hoarse whisper.

"Hungry," she said.

"Holy shit!" said the man behind me. His voice was

rising, chiming through the quiet streets like a dinner bell.

The woman's body moved involuntarily as the hunger made her shift toward the man.

"She's a fucking Z!" Xavier shouted. "Shoot her! Shoot —"

Bob touched the stun gun to Xavier's neck and the man spasmed. Bob popped him again and Xavier went to the ground. Bob was right behind him, lashing Xavier's wrists together with duct tape, then wrapping his ankles as well. The practice was paying off. He'd trussed this pig in record time.

The woman tried to push past me and go to the food, but I grabbed her arm. She pulled and growled at me, but I threatened her with the crackle of my stun gun. She flinched and cowered.

"We have a better way," I said and pushed my safety goggles up so she could see my pale eyes.

**

We allowed the woman to follow us to the warehouse. She offered to help drag Xavier, but we told her that we had him under control. In fact, I preferred not to hand the food over to her until I was sure she could control herself. Xavier stirred once, and Bob stunned him again; we could feel the current transferring through him into us. It made the muscles in my hands twitch, but it wasn't enough to make me drop the food.

I asked the woman her name, but she couldn't recall it. I asked her when she woke up and how it happened. I wanted her to think about something other than Xavier for a few minutes. She told us her story in between gulps of air.

"I was at the campus. They sent out text alerts … that we should seek shelter. We thought maybe it was a drill. But it wasn't. A man ran into me on the green … and we fell down. He bit me, and I think he would have killed me … but my boyfriend was there and brained him with a baseball bat.

"My boyfriend. Erwin. He took me back to his apartment. I don't remember much of what happened there ... but when I woke up in the apartment, I headed downtown. There were ... zombies everywhere. I guess that's what they are. What we are. Zombies, right?"

"A rose by any other name," Bob said, and I told her he was a poet.

She didn't laugh, but I could tell that she recognized the humor in that.

Xavier stirred and Bob zapped him again. My fingers twitched with the current. We were close to the warehouse now. We wouldn't need to hit the man again before he was secured.

"We eat people," I said. "Bob and I have a process that works for us."

She nodded. "I haven't had hot food ... since I woke up. Two days, I think. I ate some leftovers, but not much."

Bob grunted. "Food won't last as long with three of us."

He tapped the stun gun against his holster, and I understood that he thought we should shoot the woman.

"She'll be useful," I said.

I lied to Bob often.

**

CHAPTER TWENTY-THREE: THE SQUEAKING GOBLIN

Jane drew the next black rock in the junkyard's lottery, and she didn't argue when Maxwell encouraged her to go.

"You can see for yourself how Joey's doing," he said.

Jane stared at the rock for several seconds, recalling suddenly the title of one of the Doc Savage books in the storage room: "Death is a Round Black Spot." She tossed the stone back to Maxwell, nodded, and accepted the handshakes and congratulations from the rest of the group.

She slept very little that night, imagining the journey ahead, conversations with Dan and his crew, reuniting with Joey and the others. She hoped to see Dan's face uncovered, look into his eyes, and thank him for his service. She wondered if she could join him, earn a suit of her own and return into the wild to kill Zs and rescue survivors. She'd be the Tonto to his Lone Ranger, the Margo Lane to his Shadow. She wondered what he would smell like when he was out of uniform, and whether he had a girlfriend back home.

Before sunrise, Jane stripped off her coveralls and put on the leather biker suit, then slid a larger set of coveralls over that. Laced her sneakers. Sat on the bench seat where she slept and cradled George in both hands. She would feel naked without George dangling from her wrist, but she understood Dan's insistence against bringing weapons. She set George in the seat and left the bus for the last time.

A blood red sky glowed in the east as Jane went out to meet Dan at last. She stopped in the middle of the street and turned toward the junk wall, trying to spot Maxwell on his perch atop the dump truck. He was a lighter shade moving against the greater darkness, and she couldn't make out whether he had raised a hand to wave. Even so, she knew he must have. She raised her right hand, her back to the cowboy, and saluted the Indian. She kept her hand high until it was uncomfortable, and she held it another few breaths beyond.

We'll meet again, she thought.

Jane turned and walked toward Dan, barely able to make him out in the darkness of the alleyway. He was tall, and the duster made him appear imposing. She wondered again what he looked like under all that gear, and what sort of man could brave the wild zones with just a few guns and an experimental suit. His glasses obscured his eyes from her view. He didn't speak, instead pointing her along the alley; she looked in that direction and saw another man dressed similarly to Dan standing at the next corner, his shadow limned in a red glow of sunlight.

A gold and black Labrador paced circles in the street, keeping its eyes on Jane. She recalled seeing the dog near Dan that day she first spotted him.

As she walked toward the second man, Jane heard Dan stage-whisper, "Keep a few yards between us. Don't talk. Follow Bob unless he signals you to wait or run."

Jane nodded and plodded after Bob.

The going was slow, methodical. Bob would gesture

for them to wait before he turned a corner, giving him time to look for Zs, then signal for her to proceed. She noticed Dan wasn't careful about his own rules, edging closer to her each time Bob called a halt. In her head, she mapped the course they followed, and it didn't seem a very direct route to the island bridge. She gave them the benefit of the doubt for knowing the best path through the infested zones and around the Sun King's area, however, and kept mum.

And despite everything, the danger surrounding them, the months of horror, Jane's heart swelled at the thought of Dan getting closer still. She dared a backward glance at him. Maybe he recognized her from their first encounter, she thought, and his curiosity about her rivaled hers about him. Maybe, he wondered what was under her layers of clothing, too.

In the shadows of the early morning, she couldn't tell much about him, but she noticed how he lifted and placed each boot carefully as he walked, like a man who couldn't see the ground, or whose legs had fallen asleep. His gait troubled her, but she couldn't determine why.

Dan lunged to the right suddenly, and Jane gasped. He stepped off their track with quick, sure movements, engaged a shadow lurking in the darkness under a torn awning. Jane heard the wet impact of a blunt weapon on flesh and bone, and saw the body of a male Z drop into the street. Black liquid oozed from a hole in the top of its skull.

Damn. She hadn't seen or heard the thing, but Dan felled it without hesitation. She took a breath, whispered "Thanks," and turned the next corner in pursuit of Bob.

Bob loomed over her. His stun gun sparked blue and white just before he shoved it against her ribs, but she reacted almost as quickly. The live end touched her, made her teeth clench and knees buckle, but didn't put her down.

She swung both arms against Bob's elbow, knocking

the stun gun from his grip. It clattered on the sidewalk. Jane stumbled past Bob, flattening against a brick wall, trying to understand the sudden attack. She heard the Labrador growl, and the heavy footfalls of Dan rushing to join them.

Bob grabbed her right elbow and reached for a pistol on his hip just as Dan barreled around the turn, and the two tumbled into a heap at Jane's feet. Dan's hat and glasses fell off, and the face that looked up at her was not human.

His white eyes and dried, pale skin revealed his truth.

Jane screamed. The sound turned weird, reverberating off the silent buildings. She hadn't screamed since before the world had died, and the alien noise amplified her fear.

The dog barked, but kept its distance. Dan sprang at her, clamping gloved hands on her ankles. Jane recoiled, and fell over, her right leg pulling free of Dan's grip. She kicked at Dan's face, missed, connected with his shoulder, and he growled at her, snapping his teeth together beneath the black cowl.

Dan lunged again, but his body jerked in the wrong direction, as if struck a blow from behind. A moment later, as Dan's grip broke from her other ankle, Jane heard the crack of a rifle and realized Dan had been shot.

Jane got her hands and feet under her, shoved upright, and ran. She stayed low and sprinted hard, ignoring the burn in her bad knee. The sun wasn't yet high enough to give her a clear view, and her brain felt so scrambled by the attack that she couldn't be sure *where* her flight took her, anyway. Pavement and bricks popped and spat at her, just ahead of more barking gunfire, and she realized Dan's lunge had allowed him to intercept a bullet intended for her.

What the hell was he? she thought, and she pictured the dead man who had tried to climb after her on the phone pole. Jane again heard the I.V. Guy whispering, "What about smart zombies?"

She recalled her fantasies about the gunslinger and trembled.

Jane turned into the first alley that took her out of the line of fire, and she kept running. *When things go to shit, climb*, she thought, but she realized that whatever sort of creatures Dan — and Bob? — represented would probably be able to climb too, and just because she clambered out of reach wouldn't put her out of range of their guns.

She took another turn, trying to keep out of their line of sight, and realized that — if Dan also boasted a typical Z's sense of smell — he would be able to track her. She needed to find something to throw him off her trail, and she needed to get back to the Compound to warn the others.

The others, she thought. *Oh, God. Joey. Xavier. Johnny.*

Jane wondered how many victims these creatures had fooled and killed. How many had they promised sanctuary, only to feed upon them? She fought the tears at the thought of sending Joey off with these demons. She cursed herself for crying, knew the emotion crippled her instincts, tried to clear her head.

She stopped running. Looked around. Had no idea where she was. At least the dog hadn't chased after her.

Jane took a second to catch her breath, rub her aching knee, and think about what just happened. Bob tried to stun her, but the rubber ribbing on the bike suit under her coveralls must have protected her from most of the charge. Having failed at that, a third assailant — *a sniper?* — tried to shoot her, but hit Dan instead. She wondered how many of these creatures might be working together out here.

But she had seen Dan killing Zs. Why would he do that? Competition?

Later, Jane told herself. For now, she had to run. Distance was her only hope. She concentrated on her mental map of the city, tried to recall how many turns she had taken and in which combinations. She studied the shadows to gauge direction. Jane knew she would need to go south and east to get back to the Compound, but that meant potentially walking right back into the sights of the sniper or giving Bob another chance to stun her.

So she would have to circle north, then farther to the east before heading south, come up on the Compound from its far side and enter through the bolt-hole near the junkyard's cemetery area. That's the only way she could be sure not to cross paths with Dan and his cohorts.

She stopped short when the sting of bleach caught in her sinuses. Someone had been using the chemical nearby recently. Following her nose, Jane soon spotted a handful of scattered jugs and a white stain on the sidewalk near one of the abandoned warehouse-sized buildings on the street. She ran wide of the stain, then scrubbed her hands on the wall of the next building over, hoping to leave hints of her scent there, before returning to the bleached area. With any luck, the crossed track and spoor on the opposite building would confuse any undead pursuit.

Jane lifted the collar of her coveralls and breathed through it to filter the tang of bleach, took a chance and tried the door latch. It rotated easily in her hand. The door slid open on oiled rollers, quietly, revealing a dark cavern illuminated by the red light of the rising sun through a dirty skylight high above the rafters. Chains and cables dangled from overhead, and work tables occupied the center of the room; maybe she could find something she could use as a weapon.

Jane waited for her eyes to adjust, then rolled the door shut and threw the latch to secure it. No normal Z could open the door now except by extreme accident, she thought, although her pursuers wouldn't have any trouble with a door.

But a new odor assaulted her now, a stink of rot like she seldom had smelled before. Jane's stomach lurched and her hairs stood on end.

This is bad, she thought.

Jane peered through the half light. A variety of tools were lined up deliberately on a work bench by a high wooden table that shimmered in the morning sun. A bright pink Polaroid camera sat back in a cubby hole. In one corner of the warehouse stood a stack of cans and boxes — food and other supplies. A wheelbarrow lay on its side by the stack.

This place was Dan's lair, she realized. Right where he would have brought her, if she had fallen to Bob's stun gun. She looked again at the room, the high table she now could tell was coated in gore, the cutting tools on the bench. Xavier died here, she thought. This is what really befell Johnny. And Joey?

A rattle of chains sent her rushing to position the workbench between her and the noise. A shadowed figure lurched into the pool of crimson sunlight, and Jane shrank back until the thing reached the end if a tether. It nearly fell over when the chain attached to its neck snapped taut.

It was small, half her size. A child on a chain. The leash, attached to a dog collar around its neck, dangled from somewhere up in the darkness overhead. The child moaned softly, expectantly, reaching toward Jane with tiny fingers like a baby wanting to be lifted into her arms.

Her heart sank. Her breath caught.

"Joey?"

The dead boy squeaked as he sucked in air, groaned, and stepped forward, jerking back when his chain again reached its limits. His teeth clacked together, and his fingers twitched. He trembled and croaked. His pale face and eyes in the morning's red glow appeared coated in blood.

Jane collapsed on the floor, fighting to swallow her screams. She held her knees and rocked, watching Joey echo her movements, reaching this way and that as she shifted before him.

Jane pushed her hands against her temples. She felt

like her mind had broken. This made no sense. Why keep Joey on a leash? Could Dan be trying to make Joey into a smart Z, too? She looked around the room, fearing to see Xavier or Johnny stumbling up from behind her. Could one of them have been shooting at her earlier?

Instead, she spotted the pile of bones on the far side of the room, near another exit door. Bones and pieces of clothing, caked into a coagulated mound. Jane put both hands over her mouth to choke back rising bile.

Dan would be coming here, she thought. He might not have thought to look for her here, except that her scent trail scattered in the bleach right outside the door. He was using bleach to keep mindless Zs out of his slaughter house, and while the bleach would make it difficult for him to track her, he would be stupid not to check this building when he lost her scent close by.

And Dan was anything but stupid. He could be outside right now.

Jane nearly shouted when she heard the door rattle behind her.

Someone pulled at the outside latch.

She looked up into the shadowy recesses above the rafters where the chains originated.

Climb, she thought.

**

CHAPTER TWENTY-FOUR: FLIGHT INTO FEAR

I had her by one ankle when a car slammed into my back and threw me against the pavement. She slipped away as I realized that the impact had been a bullet and not a car, after all. Bobbie had shot me. I heard more shots as Jane ran, and Bobbie continued missing.

Bob tried to get up, but Rocky had hold of his coat tail, whipping his head back and forth, growling like mad. Bob spilled back over, knocking me down again.

I fired off a shot in Rocky's direction, heard it ricochet, and the dog ran for cover.

Goons spilled from doorways and alleys, investigating the gunfire. As a crowd shambled in our direction, I grabbed Bob up by the lapels.

"Did you see where she went?" I croaked.

One of my lungs refused to fill properly, and my voice wheezed and gurgled. The bullet had punctured my right lung. I realized speaking would be a chore from now on, and I had Bobbie's faulty aim to blame.

Bob pointed, and I started down the street in that direction, now seeing the bullet holes in the brick and block and sidewalk along the way. A goon met me at the turn. He reached toward me, but his head snapped to face the alley when he caught Jane's scent. I put him down with my hammer and picked up my pace.

Bob stayed behind to knock down goons, leaving the search to me.

I lost her once, bypassing a turn she had made and backtracking. Bob and Bobbie met me at the turn. Bobbie didn't apologize, and I didn't threaten to end her. Bob had his roll of duct tape in hand.

"Let me wrap that wound," he said.

I glared at him and stalked away. The two of them fell into step behind me. Before long I began to wonder if our luck had turned, as Jane's route was taking us toward our lair. As we approached, I stopped trying to follow her spoor so the bleach spread on the street wouldn't overcome my senses. I walked past the warehouse entrance, picked up her scent on the next street.

Looking back, I saw Bob's hand on the door latch. I motioned for him to join me, but he shook his head.

"We should check," he said.

I nodded. It made sense that Jane would have noticed the bleach bottles and wondered what was inside the warehouse. Bob threw the door open and we walked into the darkness.

Joey grunted and squealed as we entered. Chains jangled when his tether clashed against them. Our shuffling footsteps sounded too loud on the concrete floor, and the sliding door slammed shut like thunder.

"Can you smell her?" I wheezed.

"No," Bobbie said. "Thanks to that bleach. Can't even smell myself."

"A rose by any other —"

Bobbie grunted. "Oh, shut up."

From outside came the rumble of a dog growling low. Rocky had trailed us here and was still trying to track our prey. I checked the work table, ensured that my tools were untouched, my notebook where I kept it.

"If she was here … she'd have killed the boy," Bobbie said.

I gave a grunt, neither affirmation nor anger. "Let's go."

**

Jane lay on her side on a steel beam, not daring to glance over the edge and see what transpired below. She listened to their voices, the scrape of metal on wood, the groans and squeaks escaping from Joey's animated corpse. Footsteps, the latch, the door sliding and sliding again, slamming, latching again. At last, only the clank of Joey pulling on his tether, moaning.

But Jane worried that Dan and his crew were trying to trick her, that they still waited inside the doorway, expecting her to show herself. She didn't know for sure, but it made sense to her that zombies could be quite patient.

After a few minutes, Joey's irregular grunts and groans grew quiet. Still, Jane waited, until even those sounds settled. Finally, she glanced over the edge — quickly, just to get an image on her retinas — before lying back and closing her eyes to process what she had seen.

Nothing. No one. Joey, standing slack and staring toward the doorway in the golden morning. Empty spaces broken by shadows of dangling chains. Dark stains on the floor, tables, benches, and walls.

She skittered down a support beam onto the sticky floor and moved on all fours to the tool bench, choosing a long-handled ball peen hammer and a machete from the utensils she found. She grabbed a strip of cloth to wrap the handles, which were slick, gummy, and black with coagulated blood.

Jane approached the boy, and Joey again got her scent. He stumbled to the end of his chain, reaching and moaning. She knew his noises would bring the others back to this abattoir if she didn't act fast.

"I'm sorry, Joey," she said.

Jane stood just outside of his reach and swung down hard with the machete, cleaving apart the boy's frontal lobes and jamming the blade in his skull. He crumpled straight to the floor without another groan, dragging the machete along with him.

Jane wanted to cry, but she was too angry, too sick. She thought about the man who had first called her "Jane," and how she had busted his head after the bite that infected him, though he had begged her not to.

Paul. She remembered. She recalled all of their names, the infected ones she had put down. Joey, like Paul, was dead now, and she thought one should remember the names of people one killed. She promised herself she would try to remember Joey as a person, not as the pathetic creature Dan had made of him.

Jane put her right foot against Joey's head, worked the machete loose.

She leaned against the devil's workbench to collect herself. She took a deep breath and immediately regretted it. She gagged and coughed, doubling over and trying to choke back her noises.

Jane glared into the depths of the room, the shadows and chains. Closer by, the evidence of killings stained the floor. Her eyes landed on a notebook open on the table. Spiral bound, with ragged handwriting, a couple of weird diagrams like flow charts. She thumbed the pages, and saw a Polaroid taped to one: a woman roped to the table with bloody stumps where her limbs should have been.

On another page, a photograph of Joey still fresh-faced and alive, though terribly frightened.

Her hands shook. Jane closed the notebook, surprised by the cartoonish red skull face on a black background that leered from the cover. She unzipped her jumpsuit and shoved the book inside, against the belly of her biker suit. She would take this back as proof, she thought. She would return to the junkyard and gather a group, and come out hunting for Dan and his zombie posse.

She went to the sliding door, eased back the latch, and slowly edged the door open just a crack. A quick glance gave her a first impression of the street before ducking back inside and leaning against the door. She let the image process behind her closed eyes and, certain she hadn't glimpsed any Zs lingering, she leaned out again for a longer look.

Nothing moved in the streets. Nothing darkened the windows of the buildings facing her. The deep shadows of dawn had evaporated, the horror of Jane's morning having failed to freeze the sun in its orbit. The day, though still young, grew brighter and warmer with the passing minutes.

She slipped through the gap, hugging the block walls of the warehouse and making for the north, at a right angle to the direction she had tried to send Dan by leaving her scent behind on the next building. Jane knew her course took her farther into Z territory, but she couldn't risk going back to the Compound yet; the gunslinger would expect her to try to warn her people, and would set up his posse along the way, lying in wait, possibly even placing booby-traps for her.

Find a safe haven, hole up, and make a plan, Jane thought. She had some time, at least. Dan wouldn't attempt to contact Maxwell again for a few days, if only to maintain the illusion of his "mission," and she knew Maxwell would not waste the walkie-talkie batteries by checking for a message any earlier than expected. Meanwhile, Dan and his helpers would neither risk attacking the Compound nor being found out for what they were by trying to speak directly to Maxwell, Jane thought; they would be patient and hope to recapture or kill her.

At the first cross-street, Jane hesitated. She put herself in Dan's oversized boots, tried to think like a predator, if not a zombie. She would split up her team, have them watch cross-streets around the warehouse. But for how long? Jane had waited a long time before climbing down from the rafter, and they might have wandered far by now, thinking she was outpacing them, trying to regain and track her scent. She crouched, weighed the probability that someone — or rather some *thing* — waited for her to cross the alley.

She glanced over her shoulder at the empty street behind her and figured her chances. Probably no worse than the risk of one of them entering the main street at any moment and spotting her.

She looked around the corner, hesitated, then sprinted to the next building over, flattened against the wall and listened. Her bad knee throbbed in time with the drums inside her ears. She heard no shouts, no squawks from a radio, no footfalls of pursuit. She kept moving, quickened her pace despite the pain in her leg, looked for another side street to take so she could duck out of sight of the warehouse.

Halfway down the block, a man-shaped thing stepped out of a transom in front of her. She barely had time to get her arms up before she slammed into him, falling and rolling away as she bowled him over.

Jane scrambled up, hopping to keep pressure off her left knee, even as the Z tried to work out what had happened to it. She didn't recognize this one. It wore no special costume, just some nameless and hapless victim of the plague. But Jane couldn't allow it to chase her or even raise a moan that might alert others; Dan and his crew could be close enough to hear.

She limped over to the Z as it got to its feet, oriented itself and turned to look for her. She brought the hammer down as hard as she could swing, dropping the creature on the sidewalk. It lay still, eyes frozen, staring into the cloudless sky.

Jane ran.

**

CHAPTER TWENTY-FIVE: THE PHANTOM CITY

Jane turned east, now. Along a wide avenue that gave her a clear view for several blocks. It would provide any Zs a clear view too, but she needed to make some distance, and to do that she must see far enough ahead to keep running.

Now north a block, then west, doubling back onto a narrow street littered with rotted bodies, abandoned cars, charcoal skeletons, dropped suitcases, spilled boxes of ruined supplies, and other relics of the dead civilization.

Slower now, and careful. She watched the doorways and the deserted vehicles, scanned the windows and the alleys as she passed. Everywhere, she found evidence of how the world had ended. Piles of bodies where someone had tried to start a pyre, or maybe where someone had made a last stand against the dead, stacking them where they fell. Pieces of bodies, where the dead had fed and then moved on. Broken windows, burned-out cars. Black stains and the stink of death.

Jane stumbled, fell to her knees in the roadway, suddenly overcome by fatigue, the throbbing agony in her left knee, and hopelessness that welled up when she thought of Joey. She gasped as her fists hit pavement, trying to catch her fall but still holding the machete and hammer in white knuckles. The asphalt tore into the heels of her hands, and the hammer skittered away from her, clanking and jangling as it bounced on the street.

It sounded like an alarm.

Her knee felt like someone had set fire to it. She lay gasping and choked back sobs. *Not now. Not yet,* she thought. She pushed up and listened.

Somewhere, something moaned, and it was not the wind.

Jane started to run again, but her bad leg kept her from making more than a couple of steps. She put down the machete and grabbed her knee with both hands. Tears obscured her vision, and she wiped her face on the back of a dirty sleeve.

Her eyes cleared, focusing on a spilled box of supplies on the curb. A gallon jug of bleach lay on its side in the box, leaving a pale stain where the liquid leaked onto the cardboard. She shoved the machete in her belt and grabbed the bottle.

About half full, she thought, then grimaced at the possibility that she remained an optimist.

Jane heard something moving in a side street, the rising guttural call of the hunger. Quickly, she splashed bleach over the place where she had fallen and where her blood and skin marked the pavement with spoor only an animal could follow. She spread the chemical across the street where she had run, then threw the plastic jug back along her trail. It clattered and spit.

Jane snatched up the hammer, and she headed farther to the east. Whatever approached, she preferred to be long gone when it arrived.

**

The sun dropped behind the tall buildings and the shadows deepened all around. Exhausted, hungry, and hurting, Jane finally stopped running. Her dry throat burned, her mouth felt gritty as a desert. The biker suit under her torn coveralls stank, slick on the interior from her sweat. Her injured knee felt pierced by a hot poker with every step. She needed to find a safe place, clean water, something to eat.

The creatures searching for her would not tire, though they would grow hungry. That much, she knew. But she should have thrown them off with the bleach, if they even followed her into this part of the city. With darkness falling, they became a secondary concern. Jane had to get to safety and rest. That meant climbing.

An eight-story brownstone on the block seemed her best bet. She found the fire escape and jumped up to grab the low rung. The ladder, encrusted with rust, did not pull down. Jane's fingers slipped and she fell hard, off balance, banging her left knee on the pavement and again clenching her teeth against a howl of pain. Tears tingled in her eyes.

She caught a whiff of something putrid, but saw nothing close. She looked around, took a breath, got into a crouch, and tried again. This time she managed a solid hold with both hands, and as she pulled herself up, the ladder creaked and extended. It shrieked, but she let it lower until it stopped, well shy of the ground. She swung her weight and grasped a higher rung with her right hand, swung again and hooked her good knee over the bottom rung.

Something yanked her left leg, which dangled below. She kept hold of the ladder, and yanked back, stifling a cry of surprise and pain. She looked down.

A zombie girl right beneath her had a grip on Jane's sneaker. The girl was on tip-toe, reaching as high as she could reach. Her white eyes stood out against the grime and black stains covering her face. She pulled hard on Jane's sneaker, mouth wide.

Jane snatched her leg up, shooting fire from her knee to her hip as the Z's skeletal fingers twitched and her black teeth snapped and clacked. Jane's left sneaker spun in the air and fell beside the Z, but Jane got both feet onto the ladder and climbed without looking back.

At the second floor landing, Jane paused to peer down. The Z still reached, still smacked its dry lips. Jane noticed the girl's school uniform of plaid skirt, white Polo, and blue blazer. She had stretchy wristbands on one arm still bright pink, yellow, and green, none of which meant very much anymore. She stepped on Jane's sneaker as she circled.

Jane felt hatred bubbling in her throat like a memory of bile. She wanted to shout at the dead girl. The pain, the frustration, the terror and anger — it overwhelmed Jane all at once. She would have spit down on Z if she could have managed a gob. Instead, she shot the girl a bird and kept climbing to the top of the building, limping every step of the way, as her left knee swelled and buckled.

It was nearly dark when Jane reached the top. She looked back down, barely able to see the zombie girl still gesturing upward in the deep shadows pooled between the buildings. She hoped the Z would forget what it was looking for when it could no longer see her on the fire escape.

Jane studied the flat roof before stepping foot up there, hurrying to check the roof access door. The handle wouldn't turn, and a locked door meant no Zs could bother her here. She wouldn't find food or water this way, but at least she could rest, and in the morning she could figure out how to get back home.

She sat on the gravel and unzipped her coveralls, drew out the notebook, tipped the pages toward the fading glow on the horizon. Almost too dark to see. She wanted to read what Dan had recorded about Joey, however, so she flipped to the page with Joey's photo. She leaned over the notebook. She read:

"... *The child stopped screaming for*

help when he finally understood that we would continue stunning him so long as he screamed. He cried for a while, but I think he stopped crying when he began to believe our promises not to eat him. Can't be sure; asked him why he stopped crying, and he only said, 'I don't know.'

'Wanted to stun him again — want him to be more forthcoming — but Bobbie asked me not to. 'You're cooking him,' she said. 'I like them raw.'

'Kid started crying again. Even after I told him we were definitely not going to eat him, he wouldn't stop. So I shocked him again, anyway.

'Bobbie doesn't understand why I want to keep the boy alive. I realized her problem isn't a lack of comprehending my reasons, but a lack of understanding why I reason in that manner at all. She possesses no curiosity about our existence whatsoever. Ranks her little above the mindless ones. She doesn't care why we 'awoke,' what subtle mechanism separates us from goons. She simply wants to employ her regained wits to be a more effective hunter.

"'What if all zombies are becoming sentient?' I asked her. 'What if every walking corpse remembers how to think?'

"She smacked her lips. 'Then we will run the world and eat it, too.'

'I consider putting her down.

'While I wrote all of the above, Bobbie walked over and bit a hunk off of Joey's right shoulder. His scream brought me out of my thoughts. She tossed him aside as he clutched at the bleeding wound. I would have to burn

that, or he could bleed to death.

"I stuck my stun gun to Bobbie's neck and juiced her, but she barely flinched.

"'What?' she said. 'I told you I was hungry.'"

Jane's eyes burned. She wiped them against her sleeve, poked the notebook back inside her coveralls and zipped up. She curled up under the arch of a roof ventilation cover, making a pillow of her arm on the gravel. She watched the night, tried to quiet her mind. No moon rose, but the Milky Way cast a cold light over the gravel roofing. Fatigue took her, and she fell right to sleep.

**

Jane awoke once in the middle of the night. Still no moon, but the stars shined brilliantly in a black sky. The gravel seemed almost to glow.

She watched a pinprick of light arcing slowly across the sweep of the Milky Way — a satellite continuing its lonely orbits, reflecting earthlight. She wondered if astronauts yet lived on the International Space Station, and if they looked down on their homeworld and wept. Perhaps they died when their supplies ran out, or they had somehow returned to this dead planet in an escape capsule.

Her eyes followed the motion of the light across the sky, moving opposite to the slow turning of the earth under her body, and she drifted back to sleep.

**

CHAPTER TWENTY-SIX: THE LAUGH OF DEATH

Men all around her.

Somehow, even as she awoke with someone pulling at her remaining sneaker, Jane knew men surrounded her. She kicked on reflex, not even awake, but she sensed the crowd of figures, and she tried to rise, hands under her body, feet back. Something cracked the side of her head and she went back down, nose digging into the gravel and hard tar.

The men laughed.

Not zombies, she thought. *Men. This is bad.*

Jane glanced up at them as if looking around a corner to spot movement or danger. Closed her eyes. Visualized six, one shifting foot to foot, one squatting and studying her, his rifle resting on his knees. Two leaned on spears, and one of them had hit her in the head, the one nearest and on her right. The fifth had fallen back on his ass when she kicked him; the others had laughed at him.

The last one stood apart and watched, arms folded. The leader. He had a pointed nose and receding chin, with brown skin cancers crossing his face. He looked like a freckled shark.

"What do you want?" she said, still lying on her face.

They laughed again.

"Just want to say hello to our neighbor," said the one on his ass, who now nudged her with one boot. "Can we borrow some sugar?"

She didn't answer. She reached for her machete and hammer, but they weren't where she had dropped them.

"Looking for these?" one of the men said, tossing the tools aside. They clattered and kicked rocks loose from the under-layer of tar.

She blinked into the morning sun, studied them as her senses cleared and she came fully awake. Paramilitary. Camouflage clothing in jungle greens and desert browns. Weapons and belts. Heavy boots. All of them with shaved heads and faces, nothing a Z could grab, and most with ugly black tattoos on their exposed arms, necks and faces.

Her bowels clenched. She realized these were the King's men, the ones Lucy escaped. How had she not heard their boots crunching gravel when they came onto the roof? How could they have sneaked up on her?

Worse, she considered, was that she had been so fatigued she hadn't realized how close she was to 32nd Street.

The leader spoke. He wore a flak jacket and a red bandana around his neck. His voice cracked like breaking wood.

"Get her on her feet, and let's have a look," he said.

Jane struggled as the men grabbed her wrists and yanked her upright, but one behind her snatched her head back, and one off to the side punched her in the gut. She doubled over and coughed, tried to vomit. One had hold of her jumpsuit shoulders and dragged her upright again, ripping the canvas at the seams.

A man with a burn covering the left side of his face grabbed her collar in both hands; he could have just yanked the zipper, but he preferred to tear the front apart.

The force caused the material to bite into her neck and shoulders, and she collapsed to her knees again, arms twisting in their grip.

She gasped, but did not call out as the men roared — *Idiots*, she thought, *the Zs will hear* — and the red journal she had hidden between her suits spun away from her, falling open at their feet. She saw a hand reach close, pick up the journal. But then screwed shut her eyes to deny the reality of hands groping her breasts through the biker outfit.

"What are you wearing?" the burned guy growled.

A hand on her throat dragged her backward, and she felt the men shredding her coveralls to get a better look at the leather suit underneath. Their vicious tugging and tearing was like being punched all over.

She wondered if this was any worse than being ripped apart by Zs.

"Hold it!" the leader said.

Jane opened her eyes, though the men had not stopped at the order. They stripped away her ruined coveralls, using knives to slice the thicker fabric. Too many hands turned her, wrenched in opposing directions. Too many blades in play under the red sun. She couldn't keep up with what was happening.

**

Dan's narrative:

Morning threatened low on the horizon, and I stood on the verge of abandoning my search. I had found and lost Jane's track several times in the night, and at that moment, the trail was cold. I caught a faint whiff of fresh bleach on the breeze and turned into the wind. To save my senses from the chemical's effects, I stopped testing for scents as I walked toward the source.

A white plastic jug in the street lay nearby a box of other household supplies, the cardboard box stained by a missing bleach jug. Someone — in my opinion, Jane — had come this way recently and poured the bleach down her path to confuse pursuit.

I angled in the direction opposite from where the jug had been tossed away from its box. I moved slowly, checking doorways and alleys, looking for accessible stairwells and fire escapes, watching for lights in upper windows of buildings along the roads. A few blocks east, I sighted of a single white sneaker with neon pink laces lying under a rusty fire escape. I picked up the shoe, sniffed it.

Jane.

My brain burned. Excitement confused with hunger. I tested the air and experienced something akin to panic when I detected the mixed scents of several humans and at least one goon. A troop of men had been here, or close by, and recently. The sensation in my head transformed from burn into brain-freeze, heavy in my forehead.

Fear. That was new.

I could not face them alone. I drew my pistols and backed deeper into the alley, hugging the morning shadows. I listened, sniffed, watched the street, and scanned windows. The cold in my brain passed, numb again.

A gunshot rang out directly overhead.

**

The loud bark of the shark-faced man's gun brought everything to a halt. It echoed among the buildings and made the morning tremble. Jane's face ground into the gravel roofing, but she grinned, imagining her evil cowboy down on the street somewhere, searching for her, and now following the thunder of the gun. Wouldn't they be surprised if Dan showed up?

That's it, dumbass, she thought. *Keep shooting. The enemy of my enemy, and all that shit.*

Jane tried to look around, but a knee on the back of her neck held her head still. Her peripheral vision showed only glimpses of boots and bits of her clothing. Drops of blood on white rock. She realized she had been cut.

Then the journal thrust into her eye line. The open

pages showed Dan's notes and a Polaroid of a woman strapped to his butcher block, legless and armless except for bloody, scorched stumps.

"What is this?" the boss man asked.

Jane coughed and tried to speak, but she could barely breathe.

"Get off of her."

The men didn't hesitate this time. All hands left her, and Jane curled into a ball. The scraping rock on her cheek felt better to her than their hands. A welcome pain, one that made sense.

The boss man's voice hissed close: "You have about three seconds to start talking."

Jane pointed at the book. "There's a Z out there — a team of them — that woke up and worked out how to pick us off."

"Zee?" one of the men asked.

"Zulu," said another. Grunts all around.

"They're smart," Jane said. "One of them was a scientist or something when he was alive, and he's experimenting on people now."

It sounded stupid. Insane. Jane tensed, expecting them to hit her. They'd never believe her. When the violence failed to descend, she kept talking.

"I stole the book from them," Jane said. "I barely escaped. They're down there, now, somewhere, hunting for me."

She shook and the sobs erupted. She hadn't cried in forever. Now she cried because she had begun to wish that she had died, or been tortured and eaten by Dan and his kin, rather than have this happen. To become a victim of living men must be worse than to join the ranks of the dead. Jane wished Dan would show up and kill all of these men, and then kill her too.

Then she noticed the silence. No laughter. No derision. No random blows to punish her for lying to them.

Something felt like it dropped down her spine and kept going, straight through to the dead heart of the planet. Something cold.

Jane looked at them, their faces drawn tight, skin pale even in the morning's crimson glow. They believed her.

"Get her on her feet," the boss man said. "We're taking her to McKenzie."

They dragged Jane upright and shoved her toward the roof access door, the one that had been locked last night. Apparently, they came up by that route. They must use these buildings, she thought. They must watch the streets. A lookout must have seen her climb up the fire escape last night, then dispatched this patrol just before dawn.

The men forced Jane to walk between them. She limped on her bad leg, and she had lost her other sneaker during the assault. She wrapped her arms around herself as if she were naked before them, and she walked barefooted and weaponless down the dark stairwell and out into the street.

Jane didn't see the schoolgirl Z that had grabbed her last evening, but she spotted her left sneaker still in the alley as they crossed; the Z must have wandered off in the night or been put down by these men.

Jane wished she was with that dead girl right now, wherever she might be.

**

Dan's narrative:

Minutes passed as I waited, wondering if one of the men had shot Jane, considering whether or not I should try to climb to the roof. The sun gained altitude, but remained below the tops of the buildings, casting the alleys in deep shadow. I knew she was close, suspected she was in trouble, hoped she would come my way so I could put her down, finally.

I heard a door opening along the street, and the tromp of heavy boots on pavement. I crouched, huddled against a Dumpster, guns at the ready. A group of humans passed the mouth of the alley: six men forcing Jane ahead of them, eastward. The men wore Army surplus fatigues, and carried rifles, ammunition belts, hunting knives — much like the man who hunted the woman weeks ago, the hunter I killed.

Jane's canvas coveralls were missing; she wore a black, leathery racing outfit instead. I speculated she had worn it under the coveralls all along, and it saved her from Bob's stun-gun. She limped, barefooted, favoring the left leg. I thought she saw me when she glanced into the alley, almost fired my guns into the group before I realized that her eyes merely fell longingly upon her sneaker.

When the sound of their feet faded, I edged to the corner and kneeled, removed my Stetson, and peeked around the corner. The men led Jane along the middle of the street, up a hill toward a brownstone two blocks away. Even at this distance, I could make out the razor wire coiled around the building, and the shapes of guards standing on the roof.

I had been lucky to arrive in the near-dark, unnoticed by the lookouts. Luck wouldn't last, as Jane had proved. I backed away, returned to the shadows, and exited the far end of the alley. Turned west, heading away from the humans.

I knew where they were taking Jane, and I had an idea of what to do next. I hoped the men would mistreat Jane like they had the other woman I'd seen being tracked by the hunter. Just for the day. Just enough to keep all of them busy.

Because by nightfall, I would have a surprise for them.

**

CHAPTER TWENTY-SEVEN: THE BOSS OF TERROR

The brownstone occupied by the King's men stood at the rise of a hill on a slight curve, and faced a single intersecting street. Jane studied the approach, tried to analyze the situation — avoid focusing on the tortures Lucy had endured here, despite the terror twisting in her gut.

From a tactical standpoint, she appreciated the three clear vantages the building enjoyed. Jane wondered what was behind the building, but as they approached she saw it was an empty, fenced-in parking lot. Dry weeds pointed from pavement cracks. Stripped cars formed a barricade on the inside of the chain link.

Trip wires and curled razor wire lined the approaches, with guards hiding behind the only opening: a spiked barrier on a greased slide rail. Ragged boards sealed the building's lower floor windows, and more armed men stood in upper windows and on the rooftop; Jane saw a couple of them grin when she looked up at them.

She felt her heart drop. This was a true fortress, and she didn't like her chances of escape. *God damn Dan,* she thought. If only he had been for real….

The men marched her through a wide front door reinforced with heavy plywood. The door shut silently, and Jane stumbled before her eyes adjusted to the gloom. She stubbed the little toe on her right foot and bit her lip to keep from crying out.

Candles lit a room at the far end of the first floor hall, but the men directed her up the stairs to her left. She climbed and thought, *So much for Rule One.* She lost count of floors, though she believed she had turned fewer than ten landings when they reached the top.

The men shoved her along the hallway toward a door where another guard waited. Like the rest, he wore a costume of Army castoffs and prison tattoos. He had pistols in shoulder holsters, a Bowie knife on his hip, and an assault rifle in a lazy one-handed grip. "Kite," he said, nodding at the man who led Jane's captors.

"Bill," Kite replied. "McKenzie will want to see this one." He handed the skull notebook to the guard, Bill, who flipped the pages.

"Don't pretend you can read," Kite said, and his men chuckled quietly.

Bill grinned at him. "Pretty pictures," he said. He opened the door, stepped inside, and pulled it shut as he entered the inner chamber, leaving them standing in the hall.

One of the men mumbled and Kite asked him to speak up.

"Nothing," the man said.

Kite stepped toward him, resting one hand on the hilt of his knife. "Something. What did you say?"

The man glanced around at the others, tried to crack a smile. "I just said 'Shut the front door.'"

Kite took another step. "And you think that's funny."

The man's lips clamped shut. He looked down, then glanced around again, and Jane could see him seeking some glimmer of approval. But the other men gave way, stepped back, and Kite closed the gap between them.

"You just got slop duty for the next ten days," Kite said. "Get out of my face."

The man nodded, turned, and hurried down the stairs.

Kite faced the others, saw Jane studying him, and stomped back over to where she stood.

Jane looked up at Kite. "I'm hungry."

"Don't care."

She grimaced. "I was bitten yesterday."

He grinned, grabbed her throat, squeezed. "I don't think you're past your 'use by' date yet."

The other men chuckled. Jane wished she could gather enough saliva to spit. Kite released her and she gasped.

She stood quietly, waiting for whatever would happen next, but determined not to surrender herself to the flow of events. Keeping her eyes downcast, she catalogued their knives, their guns. She promised herself that she would make a grab for a weapon and die before they could abuse her.

"Let me make this simple for you," he said. "It don't matter who he was before, McKenzie's the King for a reason. He put this place together. Organized us. Designed the defenses. Made the rules. Without a chain of command and unswerving loyalty, we'd be no better than you people scrounging in the rubble. You do as you're told, and you might survive a little longer."

Then the door opened and the King of 32nd Street stepped outside to join them. McKenzie, as his men called him, wasn't what Jane expected. Particularly in light of what Kite just said.

No *Road Warrior* leather fetishism, no Mohawk or piercings, no scars or tattoos. His dark hair was cut in a short, professional style, his face shaved and clean. Mid to late 30s. He wore a black Polo shirt over bootcut jeans and a pair of white Nikes. The nails on the hand that held

Dan's notebook looked recently manicured. Not even six feet tall. Brown eyes, large and round, set in a face with high cheekbones and a hero's jaw. He almost looked familiar, like someone Jane had seen on television. Not a star, but in supporting roles. Best Friend's Boyfriend. Guy At Coffee Shop.

He waved the notebook, and Jane smelled Old Spice. "I read a bit of this."

"It's for real, I —" Jane said.

Kite slapped her face, the shock of it worse than the impact. Jane gasped and fought back tears, unwilling to show them that they had hurt her.

McKenzie nodded at Kite, acknowledging his show of strength. Then he touched the notebook to Jane's chin and tipped her red face upward.

"I am King here. You are merely a woman," McKenzie said. "Don't speak to me unless I ask you a direct question. In fact, don't worry your pretty little shaved head about anything." He looked at the gathered men, grinned at a sudden thought, and added, "Although, when I show you what I have downstairs, you have my permission to scream."

McKenzie motioned and his personal guard led the way down the stairs. The other troops dispersed to various floors as they descended, except for Kite and one other, the burned man, who kept poking Jane in the back with the muzzle of his assault rifle.

Two floors down, McKenzie paused and turned a deadbolt to open a door off the central hall. He motioned for Jane to approach, and she edged forward far enough to see into the room. The morning light angled through spaces between wooden planks covering the windows, casting a soft glow on the scene.

Several naked women looked up from wherever they had huddled on the floor, in corners, or on broken-down couches. Young and old ones, black and white ones, Asian ones — but to Jane, all of them looked like Lucy. One barely stirred. One didn't move at all.

"If things go well between us, then you can come back up here later and make some new friends," McKenzie said.

He closed the door, threw the bolt, and started back down the stairs. Jane followed, and the trembling in her legs was not only from pain.

The group continued to the ground floor, passing more men armed with guns and knives who stepped aside for their King. Turning along the hallway toward the kitchen area Jane had seen earlier, the group halted beside the basement door. A man standing watch at the door unlocked it upon McKenzie's approach. McKenzie waited beside the basement guard while Bill switched on electric lights and descended the stairs.

Jane marveled at the cold yellow glow illuminating the basement, but a musky smell wafted up, like wet books left to rot, and the fear returned.

"We're good down here," Bill shouted.

"I'll call you down," McKenzie told Jane. "I want to go down first so I can see your face when you get there."

Jane watched him go, steeling herself for a gunshot, a sudden blow to the head, something that would end her suffering before it could begin. She couldn't imagine a fate worse than the one Lucy had endured here, the hell of those skeletal flesh-toys upstairs. Again, she thought of Dan, the hope he had represented and the devil he turned out to be, and felt her last hopes fade.

"Bring her down!" McKenzie said.

Jane tried to turn away. "I don't want to go."

The man with the rifle slammed the muzzle into her ribs and shoved. She stumbled into the door frame, then let herself be pushed forward. She scarcely kept her footing down the stairs, stumbling into the handrail when her bare feet transitioned from rough wood to cold concrete.

The basement was large, with a low ceiling of

exposed rafters, a gray cement floor and cinderblock walls. It smelled musty and wet, with an underlying stink of decay that someone had sprayed air freshener to mask. Jane's stomach rolled.

Something clanked and grunted in the shadows at the back of the room, and Jane thought of Joey on his leash in Dan's abattoir. Like that place, the basement was dim, but no outside light penetrated. Pools of light provided by hanging electric bulbs in conical reflectors left large areas of darkness between them. Jane wondered if the electricity was what McKenzie wanted to show her — *no, that made no sense* — but she heard no generator running, just that commotion of a caged animal.

And then, as McKenzie angled one of the bulbs to the side like a showman spotlighting a treasure, Jane saw it.

It was female, or had been. Bent over a heavy work table, its arms extended to each side, tied to the opposite table legs. A ball gag held its jaws at bay. Its feet, flat on the floor, were separated at shoulder length by a pole of some kind attached to ankle cuffs. It was naked, gray as the floor, and pocked with cigarette burns and welts. It struggled and pulled at its bindings, and its milky eyes turned to each of the men — and Jane — in turn, promising death.

Jane lurched and heaved, gasped, and spit up green bile.

"We found this one a few days back," McKenzie said. "The men have had some fun at its expense. You probably don't want the details."

McKenzie leaned close to the zombie, thumped two fingers against the ball gag. "It just wouldn't shut up," he said. "Not that it ever cried or screamed. It just kept going, 'Rip you! Tear you! Eat you!' It became … tiresome."

He slapped the creature in the face with the notebook. It growled around the gag, and black ooze shot from its nose.

"Disgusting thing," McKenzie said, "but some of the

fellows have taken a special liking to it."

Jane looked him in the eye, and she hoped the hatred in her glare reminded him of the captive Z.

"Why am I here?" she said.

The rifle man moved to strike Jane, but McKenzie stopped him with a snap of his fingers. "I'll allow the question," McKenzie said, stepping closer to Jane.

He examined her as if for the first time. Jane matched him look for look. He stepped back, pointing at the Z with Dan's notebook.

"We thought she was a fluke," he said. "A curiosity. A freak among freaks. Now you say there are others, and you bring proof that the Zulus are conspiring. I can't abide that."

McKenzie turned away from Jane to speak to the room, for the benefit of the other men. "So, we will arm up, and you will lead us to them. And when they're dead, you'll take us to your group at the junkyard."

Jane blanched. "I don't know any junkyard —"

The rifle butt caught her in the stomach and breath burst from her lungs. She fell hard, flailed on the floor. Boots scuffled on the concrete close to her head. Tears kept her from seeing McKenzie when he kneeled beside her and spoke gently.

"I read about it in this notebook," he said. "Just the highlights, you know, but I'm a quick study. So now, we are going to go make plans and gather our gear. We'll attack the Zulus in the morning. Meanwhile, since you like to lie, you can lie down here in the dark with our talkative friend and reconsider your future. I think you'll change your tune."

McKenzie stood and Jane glared up at him.

"Remove the gag, boys," he said, and before Jane could prepare herself for the impact, he kicked her in the stomach. "Keep in mind, Jane, this is a limited time offer."

His leg went back again, and Jane clenched her muscles. The second kick rolled her over. Everything else spun sideways and faded to black.

**

CHAPTER TWENTY-EIGHT: THE SPOOK LEGION

I conferred by radio with Bob and Bobbie, giving them the specifics of the soldiers' headquarters and my orders for how to proceed, then I made my way back to the big box store, picking up followers along the way. They crawled out of doorways, climbed out of cars, lurched up from gutters at my passing. I did not shoot them or brain them with a hammer. Instead, I gestured and groaned often enough to hold their attention.

Like me, neither Bob nor Bobbie found food during their search for Jane. Since Maxwell wouldn't expect to hear from us for another couple of days, we would need to feed before we arranged for another of his group to join us. Luckily, Jane had led me to a building full of food, a brownstone-covered can of worms for the dead. I merely required some help to open the can.

The parking lot at the warehouse store swarmed with restless goons. More than when I last raided the pantry. I wondered if some humans had tried to hole up here in my absence, only to be overrun. If so, their tragedy was my profit. I nearly smiled as I drew one of my pistols and fired into the air.

The slack faces turned as one, milky eyes focused on the source of the blast. One of the nearest investigated me, shuffling close enough to sniff my clothing. When I turned to walk away, it fell in step behind me. The others that had trailed me here now heeled about and joined us, and the ones in the parking lot likewise drew into our wake. Just like that, I became the grim drum major to a hellish marching band whose only instruments were their throats.

My occasional hand-waving and shouts kept the herd in forward motion. They groaned and hissed at my back, their eyes searching ahead in mindless expectation of glimpsing whatever it was that they thought I must have seen, heard, or smelled. I was leading them somewhere, after all. There must be food.

They shadowed me from the big box store to the Interstate, picking up more stragglers as we advanced. I almost lost them when I paused to raid a police car for more ammunition; their attention wandered easily, and when I paused, they drifted away. It required effort and noise to regain momentum.

After noon, we spiraled down the exit ramp and circled through the business district. Ragged creatures crept from shadows, tottered out of dark buildings. They arose from crumpled heaps of cold bodies where they had lain in wait for so long that the congealed blood on their limbs and faces tore rotted skin from their victims when they got up.

Skin fluttered like moth wings on a bug light as they joined my army.

The sun was low, and our shadows raced ahead of us when I turned to consider the mob I had managed to raise. I dared not pause again, as we rounded a corner onto 32nd Street. Their forward motion would have continued long enough to trample me underfoot if I faltered. Instead, I gradually slowed my pace, let a few of them take the lead. I would not know if Bob had been as successful in the recruitment expedition I had assigned him until we were all well within shooting range of the brownstone.

By then, it would be too late to turn back.

**

Jane awoke on the floor in the dark. She trembled. Her body ached from the bones out. Skin felt burned and dry, belly drawn and empty, brain throbbing with pain that made lights dance in her vision. She needed water, food, rest. Probably needed medical attention.

She gasped, unsure for a moment where she was. The she heard the zombie woman growl and twitch, the ropes creak and the table pop as the Z pulled at its bonds.

"Kill you. Eat you. Eat you all," the creature hissed.

Jane realized King McKenzie and his guards had abandoned her, switched off the electricity, leaving her to suffer in the dark. As her eyes adjusted, Jane saw the merest sliver of light through the warped door frame at the top of the basement stairs. A shadow moved across the tiny beam as someone passed in the hallway.

Maybe the men would return, she thought. If she had only blacked out for a few seconds, they might still linger up there, waiting to hear her scream. Maybe they expected her to find a weapon and kill the Z woman, and they listened for the sudden silence that would indicate Jane had brained the creature.

But after minutes passed with nothing but the dead woman's thrashing and litany of murders to fill the void, Jane rolled onto her hands and knees, faced the monster in the darkness, and whistled.

"Shut the fuck up already," Jane said.

The Z fell silent and still, except for a gurgling hiss and the protesting creaks of the table under her weight.

"Eat you," the Z began. "Eat —"

"Hey! I'm getting out of here," Jane said. "If you want out too, then you'll do what I tell you."

The Z hissed. Then the hissing stopped.

"I'm listening," said a gravelly voice.

"I'll need some of your rope," Jane said. "That means I have to trust you not to grab me when I untie your hand."

The voice moaned. "I'm not really … the trustworthy type."

"Dammit. Do we have a deal?"

Silence. Jane wondered how long it took a dead brain to make decisions.

The Z croaked. "We do … if you can believe that."

Jane eyed at the door, the shadow hovering in the crack of illumination. "How long do we have until they come back?" she asked.

"The hell should I know?"

Jane clenched her fists and growled back, "Best guess."

"Pretty Boy said he'd attack someone … in the morning. You were out a while, but I don't think it's dark yet."

Not yet nightfall. Jane knew McKenzie would come for her before the excursion, expecting the Z's nonstop threats to have worn down her resolve. He would try to get her to advise him about Dan's lair. Which meant he might return at any minute.

"About 'Pretty Boy,'" Jane said. "Why do I recognize him?"

"Infomercials. Shopping channel. Had a catch-phrase."

"Shut the front door," Jane said, recalling what the soldier had said upstairs. "I'll be damned."

"No doubt."

"Okay," Jane said, "you should probably keep up your threats so they know we're not planning anything down here."

"Eat your liver, your brains, your heart!" the Z replied.

As the dead woman cursed her, Jane stood and slid her bare feet over the rough concrete floor, aiming toward the crack of light above. Her hands reached blindly for the stair rail, but her toes found the bottom step first, and the one she stubbed earlier reminded her of its injury with a jolt. She clenched her fists again, grunted at the pain.

Jane grabbed the rail and crept up the stairs, wincing with each creak of wood and listening for signs of a hand on the deadbolt. At the top of the stairs, Jane patted the exposed joists until she found the light switch. She turned on the lights and cringed, expecting the guard to notice the glow extending under the door and onto the hallway floor.

If he opened the door now, she'd have no choice but to fight. She imagined pulling him off balance and tumbling him down the stairs, and the gears in her brain engaged.

The door didn't open.

Jane nodded to herself. The men had left her hands and feet free, so certainly they must have expected her to find the lights. What they couldn't expect was Jane, herself.

After several seconds, Jane eased down the stairs. She circled the basement, searching for anything she could use as a weapon. The room was bare except for the creature in its midst. Jane returned to the table and faced the captive zombie, who ended its rant with a slow moaning exhalation that smelled of eggs.

"My name is Jane. What's yours?" Jane asked.

It gulped air. "I don't remember." Gulped again. "The men call me Honey."

Jane's skin crawled, and she wondered if that was exactly the effect the creature hoped to provoke. Up close, she could see how its skin was drying, cracked and peeling. Clear fluid seeped from welts left by whipping and dozens of small burns. Bone showed in a couple of places on top of its head, where its hair was missing and scalp was torn. Jane couldn't guess its age before it died.

Jane kneeled beside the table and started working the knot on the woman's left wrist.

"I had an aunt named Prudence," Jane said. "Clammy

and hateful bitch. She dipped snuff. You remind me of her."

"She must have been awful."

Jane nodded as Prudence returned to her loud ranting. Jane's fingers touched Prudence's chaffed skin, which wrinkled and pulled free as Jane worked the rope, exposing gray meat beneath. Jane choked back a reflexive gag.

"Okay, you're almost loose on this side," Jane said. "You need to be still when this releases. No unusual noises. No sudden moves. Don't give them a reason to come down here."

"I imagine you would … scream if I tried anything," Prudence said between gulps of air.

"At least."

"Good. I like a screamer."

Jane turned the last knot under her finger, slid the rope through, and Prudence's wrist came loose. The other was still tied, but the creature stood half-erect with a wet sound of cracking joints and stretching sinew. Jane flinched, seeing the flattened, hardened flesh of its chest, where black blood had pooled while it lay on the table.

Prudence flexed her fingers. "Now the other," she said.

The ceiling thundered with the passing of booted feet. Men mobilizing. Jane listened, and wondered if time ran faster here than in the junkyard, where days lasted forever. She crouched and untied the other end of the first rope, wrapped around a table leg. From this vantage, she got a clear look at Prudence's foot shackles, the black stains of dried zombie blood that had run down her legs. Jane tried not to retch.

"You won't get far in those ankle cuffs," Jane said. "We need the key."

Prudence groaned, then took in air. "The guard on the door has it. He's used it before to … rearrange me."

Jane swallowed. What the hell was she doing? This

creature would kill and eat her if she set it free — but the men upstairs would rape and torture her if she didn't escape. They might take down Dan and his cohorts first, if she told them all she knew about the Z slaughterhouse, but their next stop would be her friends at the junkyard Compound. Jane couldn't allow that, or even dare lead them in that general direction.

She had one mission, to protect her people. That meant breaking free, warning Maxwell and the others, and helping them bug out before Dan or these crazy men came calling.

"Get ready," Jane said.

She quickly circled the room, removing the bulbs from all except the one light pointing at Prudence. *Battery power*, she thought, then decided it didn't matter.

Jane took the length of rope she'd liberated and tied it about shin-high, three steps down from the top of the stairs, securing one end to an exposed wall joist and the other to the upright support for the stair railing. She didn't plan to leave the rope there, but if someone came in before she was ready, tripping him might give her a few seconds to get to his gun.

Jane looked back and saw Prudence pulling at the knots on her right wrist.

"Hold on," Jane said. "We either get out of here together, or I die and you stay tied up for their fun and games."

Prudence huffed and glared at Jane.

Jane returned to the table and gave the Z another appraisal. The creature mirrored her stare. If Prudence attacked, Jane wondered, could she fight it off? It's one thing to kill a dumb Z, but a Z that's as smart as you? Jane blew out a breath and wondered what Prudence was thinking.

"I'm going to remove this second rope," Jane said. "You need to stay right where you are and pretend to still be tied to the table. Lie back down. When the guard comes in, he needs to think you're still secure. If I can't take him out, then that's the only way to get him close enough for you to attack."

Jane kneeled and started noodling the rope on Prudence's right wrist. Prudence lay down on the table, her eyes on Jane. She was fully close enough to lunge and bite Jane's hand, near enough to grab at Jane's clothes with her free hand and sink those blackened teeth into Jane's throat.

Prudence swallowed air and said, "You smell delicious."

Jane paused and scowled at the creature's impassive face. She pointed toward the other side of the table. "Face that way. If you move again, we're done here."

Prudence turned away, put her cheek on the table. She took a wheezing breath. "You are either the bravest or dumbest person ever."

**

CHAPTER TWENTY-NINE: WAVES OF DEATH

My legion of doom ascended the rise toward the human stronghold, stumbling forward in the general direction I led them. Shadows moved in the upper windows of the brownstone, where the goons would not think to look without some cause. I slowed even more, allowing the mob to brush past me in its inexorable march, but without a determined leader, their pace immediately slackened. They might soon lose interest in the march and wander off on their own.

Just then, we heard the answering moans of other goons mounting the opposing side of the hill. I wondered what terrible fear coursed through the men in their high tower at the sight of the approaching armies, the echoing resonance of their hungry call, the vibration of their feet upon the pavement — and I confess I felt a moment's excitement like a dull reflection of beautiful hunger burning in my face.

The two groups sighted one another, and increased their gait, seemingly convinced in their limited way that food must be here — else why would all these others be hunting? I continued to drop back behind the crowd, as I suspected Bob would do, but not without spotting the moment when the leader of his mob caught the scent of living people, a heady aroma of sweat, feces, and blood. It was a female, freshly turned if her condition was any indication: Her jeans and blouse bright and clean, her brown face unmarked by rip or rot. Her nose lifted, her face rotated toward the building, and her pale eyes focused with clear determination.

She angled toward the brownstone, and her herd followed. Mine fell in among them, and I saw the first of them drop before I heard the crack of the shot. The humans inside the building had waited to engage the army of dead. Perhaps they hoped the herds would just pass them by. But now, with the goons fairly beating on the front door, they opened up with guns from the high windows and the rooftop.

Bodies fell and tried to rise, but those advancing from the rear stamped them into the pavement. Goons hung up on razor wire, but the pressing mob tramped over them. More fell to gunfire, and more used the fallen as a carpet across the razor wire. As the initial panic faded from the shooters, their aim improved, and head-shots took a toll. Even with the strength of numbers, if the goons found no clear way inside, then they would lose to the men with the guns.

Full dark was on us when a missile streaked overhead, fired from the top of a building down the intersecting street. Rocket-propelled grenade. It connected with the front doors of the tower in a flash of brimstone that shook the block. Bobbie had held up her end of my scheme, and gathered the bazooka from the National Guard truck I raided on my second day awake. Her attack could have been better timed, but at least on this occasion her aim was true.

The brownstone wall facing the street exploded and crumbled, throwing several of the goons backward and shredding the few in the lead. The rest continued forward, drawn by the flames, men screaming inside the structure, and the strong, sweet stench of spilled blood and burned flesh. They pushed through the broken doors and entered the ruined building.

**

The basement shook and fine debris rained down on Jane. Shouts and screams carried through the ceiling from above.

The door at the top of the basement stairs opened into the darkness. The guard, a silhouette rimmed in drifting dust and smoke, reached in and hit the light switch. One bulb flickered to life, angled at Prudence. All else remained black, and Prudence lay silent, a still life portrait of death on a table.

"Come out, girl!" the guard shouted, holding the door open with one foot. "Get up here!"

Gunfire erupted from somewhere behind him, and the guard glanced over his shoulder, out into the hallway. Whatever he saw made him slip inside and slam the basement door behind him. He put the key in the deadbolt lock and turned it. Backed away from the door, two steps down the stairs. Halted, gun aimed at the door.

He waited, listened. Through the walls issued the din of fighting. Bullets, screams, bodies thrashing on floorboards.

The man grunted and drew a penlight out of one of the cargo pockets on his pants. He turned and shined it around the room, but he couldn't find Jane. He leaned over the rail to look in the space under the stairs, where a lurker might lie in wait.

Nothing.

He stood upright, and Jane reached down from the rafter where she had been watching him. She looped a rope noose fashioned from Prudence's bonds around the guard's neck, and yanked it tight across the rafter. Gripping the other end of the rope, Jane swung down onto the stairs above the guard, kicking him down the steps.

His penlight spun across the floor. His rifle clattered the other way, and Prudence hissed up at them.

Grasping at the noose, the man stumbled back, tripped on the rope Jane had tied across the stair, and as he fell the noose went taut. His neck made a loud *pop*.

Jane pounced, knees-first, dropping her weight against him. The rope snapped tight again. He jerked and grunted. Blood spurted from his nose, and he lay still, half-supported off the stairs by the noose.

"Bring him to me!" Prudence growled.

Jane looked down from the stairs. Prudence hobbled away from the table, her ankles still cuffed to the bar, her shadow elongated in the single ray of light. Beneath the gurgle of blood and air in the guard's lungs, a rumble like heavy traffic in the street made the stairs vibrate.

Jane stood, grasped the stair rail and jumped up, landing her good knee on the guard's ribcage. Bones cracked and air huffed from his throat. His body shuddered. He stared at the rafters and wheezed once.

Jane scrambled down the stairs, snatched up the rifle, and aimed at Prudence.

"Back off," Jane said. "You can have him, but I need him first."

Prudence hissed again, bared her teeth. She hovered over the guard for a moment, clearly considering the choice, then hobbled backward and used the table to balance while she watched and waited.

From upstairs came the crack of gunfire, the crashing of a stampede in the halls.

Jane searched the guard's pockets. She stripped off his flak jacket, boots and ammunition belt. The boots were a couple of sizes too big, but she used the man's knife to cut off his pants legs, and she wrapped her feet to make the boots fit better. She slung his rifle over her shoulder, chambered a round in his pistol, holstered it on her right thigh and strapped his hunting knife's sheath to her left one.

Prudence didn't speak or move the whole time.

"You've been patient," Jane said.

"You've been lucky. The building is overrun, and his blood smells so good ... I want to eat both of you."

Jane raised the pistol, aimed at Prudence's face. Jane could end her, but the barking gun would either bring more men or excite the Zs upstairs. Jane fingered the hilt of the knife on her hip, thinking she could put Prudence down almost as easily with it.

"We had a deal," Prudence said.

"You're a fucking zombie."

"Literally," Prudence said. "What's your point?"

Jane choked back bile. What these men had done to Prudence was worse than anything the Zs could manage, she thought. Except possibly Dan. She lowered the gun, moved away from the guard's body, mounted the stairs.

"If anyone asks about me, tell them you ate me," Jane said. She removed the door key from the ring, tossed the rest of the keys down to Prudence.

"It could still happen," Prudence said.

Jane unlocked the door. "*Bon appetit*," she said.

Then the door exploded inward with a clap of thunder, propelled by smoke and flame, and Jane barely had a moment to raise her hands before impact and darkness took her.

**

Dan's narrative:

A second explosion ripped through the building, and a portion of the upper floors collapsed along the back wall. I wondered if the fire had ignited the humans' ammunition depot or if a defender had decided to use a grenade to kill himself rather than be eaten alive. Either way, it was over for this nest of vipers. My hungry ferrets would tear their refuge apart, devour the meat within, break the bones, and suck out the marrow.

I waited in an alley, wrestling with my own desire to join the buffet, listening as the screams grew more desperate.

Again, staccato barks of gunfire erupted as the surviving humans fought to repel the mob. Automatic weapons tore into the crowd but couldn't stop the forward movement. Too much confusion, too few head shots. Those knocked down by body shots just got back up and continued marching.

Another wave of goons washed through the burning gap at the front of the building, their shadows creating obscene figures in the smoke. Several armed men struggled against them with rapid fire rifles at the foot of the stairs, but even from where I stood and watched, I knew the men were goners. We had the numbers and cannon fodder to spare.

A tattooed man in camouflage tried to escape through the broken wall, but the goons tore him apart. I saw no others attempt to flee, and marveled at the unstoppable force that climbed and crawled and strode through the breach in the burning rubble to the building's wrecked interior. The human defenders had no hope now. At best, a few might survive by bolting themselves in an interior room and waiting out the invasion.

They didn't count on me to come knocking.

Only after the noise of gunfire had all but silenced itself, I approached the brownstone. The chorus of moans from within the building told me the goon army feasted. I stepped over bodies and parts of bodies that had been our first wave, negotiated chunks of wall scattered in the street, and considered the flames burning overhead. The structure, compromised by explosion and fire, could collapse at any moment, but I wanted to know that Jane was dead.

Had to know. Survival depended on it.

Bob joined me on the front steps, guns in both hands. "Once more unto the breach, dear friend?"

I shook my head. "Not yet. Cover this side. I'll circle around. Take no chances. Shoot to kill. Feed later."

Rubble and the constant distraction of blood-scent in the air slowed my progress. I passed a shattered window, smoke billowing out between wooden slats. Heard a woman's cry from a room above me where fire raged. Continued walking.

The rear of the structure faced an empty lot where a building had been demolished some years ago — its outline still visible in the earth had become a fenced parking lot, and the humans had used it for a rear approach to their headquarters. Here, the brownstone's upper floors had crumbled to heaps of brick and mortar. Tendrils of smoke twisted from a massive crack in the lower wall, lighter than the billows roiling in front of the brownstone; the fire had not yet spread this way.

I clambered up the slope of debris from the fallen walls, stepped through the crack, guns up. Unhurt by the smoke, my eyes quickly adjusted to the gloom, picking out movement in the glow of firelight through broken walls and ceilings. Goons dined in knots of twitching arms and legs, faces buried in the torsos of dying men. I ached to join them, but my long-term survival required that I find Jane and my Red Skull notebook. So I edged around the piles of bodies and the feeders.

To my left, a blasted doorway revealed broken stairs leading downward into darkness, covered in rubble. To my right, closer to the front entrance, stairs led upward.

If Jane was here, I thought, the men would have taken her upstairs. Their leader would be up there, farthest from attack. That's where the bark of guns still called the diners to feed. I put my shoulder against the wall, peered upward into smoke and orange flickers of firelight, and eased up the stairs, stepping over or upon the corpses of my army.

**

CHAPTER THIRTY: NO LIGHT TO DIE BY

Jane awoke on the basement stairs, ears ringing, body aching. She felt the guard's corpse under her; he had broken her fall while the basement door spun aside, taking out the stair rails. She looked past her feet toward the top of the steps, where smoke billowed into the basement space, filling the rafters and edging lower. Distorted shadows moved through the smoke upstairs, accompanied by banshee wails and moans of the dying and the undead. Jane's eardrums pounded, muffling the sounds. Everything seemed far away.

Jane spun to look for Prudence, and the motion made her head swim. Her vision blurred, and she clutched at the wall joist to her right as the world tumbled. She tried to wrap her head around what had happened. A second explosion? Must have been dazed only seconds, she thought, or else Prudence surely would have bitten into her — fresh food.

The one remaining light was dead, and Jane couldn't see or hear anything in the darkness below her. She wondered if the falling door struck down Prudence.

The creature was somewhere in the dark, and the thought made Jane feel for the rifle she'd been carrying. She reached all around, coughing as dust and dirt cascaded off her face and clothing.

No rifle.

The ceiling shook and more dust and bits of brick rained on her. Jane hacked, felt the building tremble as if struggling to stay erect. It vibrated from its crown to its foundation, and Jane shook too.

For a moment, light filled her vision as the upper wall gave way. Mortar and chunks of drywall dropped like an avalanche down the stairs, pouring over Jane. Bodies and bits of burning wood rolled across her onto the basement floor. The stairs shifted, rail side dropping toward the floor, dumping rubble, the living and the dead. Jane fell too, slamming into the debris, feeling more striking her as she went.

Jane looked up in time to see a soldier rising out of the ruins, grappling with a Z. Both of them shimmered, firelight reflecting on blood. Other forms emerged from the smoke and dust, converging on Jane. She reached for the pistol on her hip, but the holster was empty. Scooting backward, sliding her feet beneath her so she could stand, she found the knife still in its sheath and drew it.

Gunshots cracked, too loud in the enclosed space, and Jane ducked. From her left, Prudence strode naked out of the shadows and into the fray, hair wild, rifle butt tucked into her shoulder, squeezing off rounds in twos and threes.

The soldier fell, and the Z with him, collapsing into each other's arms. The others, only shadows in the smoke, went down too. Those that tried to rise caught more bullets, headshots, and lay still.

Prudence turned the weapon on Jane, and grinned. "I remember what I did before," Prudence said, sighting along the barrel. "Care to guess?"

Jane didn't flinch away, though inwardly she braced

for the impact.

Prudence wheezed and used the gun to motion up the hill of debris. "Go! Go now!"

Jane went. She scrambled on all fours up the brick and twisted wreckage, past arms and legs jutting at strange angles from the rubble. The collapse broke the building's back and destroyed the basement stairs, but the fallen debris formed a ramp Jane could climb.

The bricks scattered, rolled under Jane's feet. She slid backward, but grasped one of the jutting limbs like a root on a hillside. She used the cold flesh and bone to pull herself up the incline. Head down, Jane made it to the first floor, and to a crack in the back wall, an open space beyond the fire.

A man stumbled toward her out of the smoke and flames, clambering across the bricks and bodies toward Jane. He had one arm and a ruined face. She climbed to meet him, leading with her knife. She plunged it into his open wound of a mouth, and he dropped backward. Jane yanked the knife free as he fell.

She kept moving, not knowing if he was a Z or merely an injured soldier. She slipped through the gash in the back wall. Skittered down a slope of bricks wet with blood and the septic tank stench of draining pipes. Took a knee on the level parking lot, caught her breath, and glanced back at the destruction.

Shadows moved in smoke, screams answered sporadic gunfire. A wall caved in somewhere on a higher floor, and sparks spiraled into the night. Whatever remained inside that place was dead, or as good as.

Jane sprinted away from the pyre, cursing in her head every time her left knee protested, with only two thoughts.

Alive. Free.

**

Dan's narrative:

The stairs, crowded with goon corpses and lighted only by the glow of flames in other parts of the building, made the climb laborious. I planted my boots with care before stepping higher, finally holstering one pistol so I could grasp the railing for support.

The second floor was a carpet of motionless corpses, fallen wallboards, and spreading fire, with no access to the rooms beyond the landing. I resolved to climb faster. On the third floor, a group of half-starved women had died badly, and more goons than I could count writhed in thick smoke and flickering firelight, pulling and gnawing their body parts.

On the fourth floor, a man shot at me from the landing. His bullets flew wide, and I returned fire. He shouted an apology.

"I thought you were Zulu," he said, stepping from cover. "Is it clear below?"

I waved him closer, and we each took a step. I leveled my pistol and fired until he stopped twitching, not willing to risk more return fire.

Goon moans answered from floors above and below, and in moments a group of them pressed past me on the stairs, eyeing me as they stumbled over one another to get to the fresh corpse.

The fifth floor was as high as I could continue. The stairs above had collapsed outward with a portion of the wall, and only gaping spaces pierced by broken joists hung overhead, roiling with smoke that glowed orange with flame. A pile of goon bodies outside a broken doorway lured me closer, seeming to indicate a massive firefight had erupted here before numbers overwhelmed the defense.

I pressed against the door frame and glanced around the corner. A mass of goons feasted in the open space of a large communal room, where men had overturned tables in a futile attempt to slow the advancing horde. Three dead soldiers lay together by a secondary door on one side of the room, and though goons now tore at their corpses, I could see that they had shot themselves in the head.

I wondered what treasure they protected before

surrendering to the darkness.

I tried the doorknob, and it turned, but the bodies and the press of goons feeding on them blocked it from opening. Grabbing one corpse by the heels, I dragged it aside, the goons crawling along to keep hold of their warm meal.

I spun the doorknob and yanked, shoving the torso of a second body out of the way, and the goons with it. They regarded me only a second before burying their faces in the soldier's meat.

The door revealed a closet space, where a man crouched in the dark corner, his black Polo shirt covered with blood and brain matter. By his side lay my notebook with the red skull face on it. I reached for the book, and the man screamed, startling me — I had mistaken him for newly dead, another suicide, but he was merely in a daze, and my approach set him off.

I grabbed the notebook, then fell into the closet as goons left their quiet meat to answer the man's scream. They rushed to crowd into the closet, pressing me against the wall. I could feel heat through the boards at my back, but the maddened goons took precedence. The man's screams excited them, and they tore at us both, indiscriminately. I tried to shove them away, but they gripped my coat sleeves and pulled me from the closet, into the room.

I tumbled in the midst of them, and one dove on me, biting into my leg. The others quickly sensed that I wasn't food and turned on the man still huddling in the closet. I put a bullet in the biter's head, which brought some of the others back to reconsider me.

I sat still and stared at them, and when they once again attacked the human, I rose to my feet. The darkness grew thick with smoke, and I had to rely on touch and memory to find my way back to the stairs. I stumbled, slipped. I fell. But I kept hold of the notebook, finally exiting through the crater of the front doors.

A female zombie sat on the stoop, pulling at one of the corpses, another of the soldiers, who had died in the initial breach. Rather than chew the remains, however, she stripped the corpse of its clothing. She saw me and reached for an AK-47 at her feet.

"Don't shoot," I said. "I'm a zombie too."

She kept the gun trained on me while I removed my hat, glasses, and scuba head gear. She lowered the gun, but I noticed her finger remained on the trigger.

"I'm not a zombie," she said.

"Do you have a name?"

She thought about it. I expected her to say that she couldn't remember her name.

She set the gun aside and returned to removing the soldier's belt. "I'm Prudence," she said. "Give me a hand with this?"

I stood beside her, opened my duster to show her the wet suit. "We'll get you something better," I said.

"Black costume? I saw a woman wearing … something like that today. The King's men brought her inside."

My brain twitched. I felt it, like a rodent in a trap. This creature had seen Jane. "Red peach fuzz hair? Where is she?"

Prudence pointed at the brownstone. Just then, the third floor imploded, joists spearing through the heart of the structure. Sparks rose and smoke swallowed the stars.

"Parts of her, anyway," Prudence said. "I ate the rest."

**

CHAPTER THIRTY-ONE: THE ANGRY GHOST

Bobbie joined Bob, Prudence, and me at the burning brownstone. She didn't speak to us, just gave Prudence a glance and sat down to eat the nearest fresh corpse. Bob and I watched. Prudence stared at Bobbie's wetsuit, then looked at me and nodded. We took turns feasting on the freshly dead and watching the exits for men trying to escape the fire and the goons. None emerged.

Prudence shadowed us at a distance, preferring to choose her own meals from among the fallen rather than sharing ours. In turn, I kept one eye on her, unsure how far I could trust her, or her story about eating Jane. I asked Bob what he thought about the woman.

Bob turned dead eyes on me, blood and bits of meat dripping from his mouth. He shrugged. "Death be not proud," he said, and returned to his food.

Throughout the night, the fire continued to draw more goons from the surrounding city blocks. Some of them tried to take our food, and we put them down. Others wandered into the building, oblivious to the danger, and mounted the stairs or shifted bricks to exhume the dead. Just before dawn, the last of the floors gave way, and the entire building collapsed upon itself, sending up embers and gray ash. If anyone had been alive inside, they were dead now.

Sated for the moment, we gathered all the weapons we could carry from the dead soldiers, and began the long hike back to my warehouse. Prudence pulled on a dead man's boots, draped a long jacket over her shoulders, and followed us at a distance. She trusted us about as much as I trusted her.

Full daylight beamed down on us by the time we reached the warehouse. A ragged goon stood by the sliding door, sniffing and pushing against the metal with skeletal fingers. I dared to take a whiff, and caught the stink of rot overwhelming the old bleach on the sidewalk. Joey was still in there, and a day's heat had done its work on him; he might have burst open by now, and I figured that's what we smelled.

I put my ball peen hammer through the goon's skull, and Bob helped me drag it aside. Rocky sniffed the corpse, but must have gotten a snort of bleach; he scrubbed his snout on the concrete and whined.

Bob opened the door, and we joined him inside. I closed the door behind us, momentarily surprised as Rocky rushed through the narrowing gap and into the warehouse.

"Dan," Bob said, and I looked in the direction he pointed.

Joey was gone. Only a black stain showed where the corpse had fallen.

"The wheelbarrow," Bob said.

It wasn't parked by the piles of supplies we had gathered. It was as absent as the boy's remains.

"Jane," I said and glared at Prudence.

She didn't react.

"You didn't kill Jane at all," I said. "She came back here, got Joey's corpse, and took it to show her friends."

"What you're saying doesn't mean anything to me," Prudence said. "Just words."

She looked at us, making no move to bring her rifle to bear.

"She's ruined everything," Bobbie said. She dropped the rifles she had toted like cordwood, chose one from the pile, and aimed it at Prudence. "She's a liar."

Now Prudence leveled her gun at Bobbie. "I made a deal," she said.

"Humans don't make deals with goons," Bob said, raising one of his pistols at the new girl.

"We're not goons, are we?" Prudence said. "I am not a zombie."

"Everyone shut up," I said. "Let me think."

That's when someone knocked three times on the outside of the sliding door and called out, "Little pig, little pig! Let me come in!"

**

Moments after her escape from the brownstone, Jane paused on the street beyond the parking lot to catch her breath and get her bearings. She pictured the map of the city in her mind's eye, plotted her fastest route back to the junkyard. She rubbed her leg, then froze as a Z tottered out of an alley no more than 20 feet away and stumbled toward the flaming beacon. Drawn by the spectacle and the aroma of roasting meat, it didn't notice her. Jane watched it go, saw others homing in on the fire from other directions, weird shadows following them toward the flame.

And as she looked back, Jane spotted a familiar silhouette standing near the pyre, his hat and duster casting an elongated shadow across the parking lot.

"Dan," she said, and realized that all of this was his doing, his attempt to kill her, to keep her from alerting her friends. He had raised a Z army and attacked the stronghold to ensure her death. If he decided to do the same to the junkyard, Jane thought, they would be overwhelmed.

She ran, hugging shadows and watching for Zs, and wondered how she would convince Maxwell and the others that her wild story was true. If she still had the journal, with its photographs of Dan's victims, they would believe her. But without it?

The thought of Joey being left on that chain like a dog made her angry, and she suddenly knew how she could convince Maxwell.

She would take what remained of Joey home.

It was nearly dawn when she turned the corner with Dan's wheelbarrow and advanced on the junk wall. Jane couldn't see the lookout, and no one shouted a challenge. Were they in trouble, she wondered, or already dead? Had Dan attacked them? Had some other terror taken them in the night?

A spotlight picked her out, and she stumbled. The blinding light surprised her; they never used one before, and she wondered if they had grown so complacent in their acceptance of Dan's help that they would chance using a light. They knew light drew Zs. So did human voices and other noises, but it didn't stop her from shouting.

"It's Jane!" she called out. "Send Maxwell out ASAP!"

The spotlight winked out. Though black spots floated in her vision, Jane saw a signal flag swing over the dump truck. In the dark, she couldn't make out the color. Seconds later, she heard Moses speaking low from the other side the junk wall.

"What the hell happened, Jane? What is that in the wheelbarrow?"

"It's Joey," she said. "Let me in."

Moses crawled through the bolt hole, but rather than letting Jane inside, he clambered out to take a closer look at the body in the cart. He trembled.

"He was a Z," Moses said. "You put him down?"

Jane nodded. "I'll explain."

Moses followed her back through the bolt hole, latching the doors as he went. Seconds later, Maxwell jogged to join them. He grabbed Jane by the shoulders, face slack, then crushed her in a bear hug. When he released her, she stepped away and looked at the others gathering around them. Willy, Ruth, Lucy — pale faces in the night with frightened eyes gleaming.

Jane pointed at the wheelbarrow and told them how she found Joey. How Bob and Dan tried to stun her, and she ran right into their lair. Her nose felt clogged, and when she wiped it, she realized her face was wet.

Maxwell tried to ask questions, but Lucy shushed him. "Let her speak," Lucy said. "Listen to her."

Jane described her flight into the city, being captured by the soldiers, and left in the basement with Prudence. Lucy reached out and took Jane's hand, and Jane let her hold fast.

"I saw them," Jane said to Lucy. "The other women. I saw."

Lucy let go of Jane's hand and wrapped herself in her own arms.

Jane told them about the explosions, the fires, the building being overwhelmed by a horde of Zs, and how she slipped away with Prudence's help — only to see Dan walking the perimeter of the building.

"Dan and his crew have been feeding on us, one at a time," Jane said. "They kept Joey chained up to see if he would turn into a smart Z like them."

"I don't understand," Maxwell said.

"He knows where we live," Jane said. "He may think I'm dead, and try to trick you into sending someone else out to him. Or he may think the junkyard is a liability, and bring another Z army here and kill all of us."

"What do we do, Jane?" Willy asked.

Jane looked at the group. Over their shoulders, she saw more faces by the inner wall, watching them closely.

She looked at Maxwell, saw his jaw clench.

"We take them out," Jane said. "We arm ourselves and go into the city to their warehouse, and we take them out."

Moses reached to open the bolt hole, and Maxwell asked where he was going.

"I will give Joey a proper burial," Moses said.

Jane thanked him. She reached to touch Maxwell's arm, but drew back.

"Dan is mine," Jane said. "Put down the others, but I want him intact."

**

Dan's narrative:

Rocky barked at the doorway, nearly drowning out the woman's voice calling to us from outside.

"There's no reason for anyone else to die today," she said.

I looked at Bob and whispered, "Jane."

Bob nodded, put his pistol to the side of his head. "Lovers to bed; 'tis almost fairy time," he said, and squeezed the trigger, splattering his black brain matter across the wall and Bobbie.

I watched him fall, failing to understand how he could have done that, or why. Rocky turned from the door and set upon Bob, sticking his snout into the smoking exit hole and gobbling.

"Who is shooting?" Jane yelled.

Another shot rang out, and Rocky yelped, twisting and flopping. I saw Bobbie lean closer and put a second bullet in him, ending his torment.

"Hate that dog," she said.

"What the hell is going on?" Jane shouted through the door.

I leveled a gun toward the door, but before I could fire, a cracking sound caught my attention, and Bobbie slumped sideways to the floor. Glass shards rained onto the concrete, and I looked up. A sniper ducked down, having shot through the skylight, and I dropped for cover behind the tool bench.

Prudence already crouched there. She drew in a gulp of air and bellowed, "Jane! We had a deal!"

Jane shouted for everyone to stop shooting, then she asked, "Who is that?"

"It's Prudence! I followed them back here. They promised me new clothes."

Silence answered, and I imagined the humans consulting with each other outside. I glared at Prudence, and her white eyes crinkled with cold humor.

"Looks like one of us is walking away from this," she said.

Jane called, "Come out, Prudence!"

Prudence pulled herself upright using the table for leverage. She scowled at the sniper, then crossed in front of the tool bench. She reached for the door handle.

Gunshots rang out.

Bobbie had been playing dead. She fired her rifle until the magazine emptied, and I saw Prudence hit the door and slide out of sight, leaving a black trail along the metal siding.

"Dammit! Who's shooting?" Jane said.

The sniper fired again, three rapid shots, and this time Bobbie wasn't playing dead.

"Prudence?" Jane said.

No voice answered her.

"Dan?" Jane called.

"I'm still here."

"It didn't have to go like this," Jane said. "I made a deal with Prudence. I'm still willing to make a deal with you. Give up, and we will not put you down. I guarantee your survival."

I looked at Bob's corpse and wondered if he had taken the right action. He'd always walked close to the exits, and had even asked me several times why I didn't simply shoot him. But then, we had reigned over hell.

Could I serve in their heaven?

My imperative remained unchanged. To survive, I would have to submit. At least, until another opportunity presented itself.

"What do you want me to do?" I said.

"Put down your weapons, take off your gear, and lie face-down on your slaughterhouse table. When our sniper gives the all-clear, we'll come in and restrain you."

"Okay."

I stood up and faced the sniper. I recognized him as one of the group that investigated my handiwork the day after Jane first spotted me. Not Johnny, obviously. The other guy.

I thought about the future, and it struck me that's another thing the dead don't do. They don't care about the future. They don't have one. But then, what kind of future would I have if I let them put me in chains?

I removed my glasses, my hat and head cover. I glanced up at the sniper, who watched me through his scope. I shrugged out of my duster. I unlatched my belt, untied my leg straps, set my pistols and ammo on the table. Reduced to the wetsuit and boots I had started with, I stepped around the tool bench. One boot caught on the strap of Prudence's dropped AK-47, and I leaned over to untangle myself.

I brought the gun up and strafed the skylight, a blast of fire and roar of barrel that ended in the shriek of breaking glass. The sniper slumped and slid out of sight.

Jane shouted my name, and I answered her.

"Dan?"

"Jane?"

I threw the door open and stepped into the morning sun, strafing left to right. People standing against the walls scattered. Blood splashed on brick and concrete. Lights flashed from all sides, and I felt impacts — much fewer than the flying bullets, but enough to knock me down. One hit my left shoulder, and I lost my grip on the rifle.

One caught my gut, and I folded over. One popped my right kneecap, my legs collapsed, and I nosed into the bleached pavement.

I tried to get my right arm under me, push upright, but a weight came down on my neck.

"Say good night," Maxwell said.

"Stop!" Jane shouted.

I tried to get air into my lungs and growl, but too many holes and too much weight on my back made breathing impossible. I saw Maxwell's shadow on the nearby wall, the shape of a big hammer in his hand.

"Tie his wrists and ankles," Jane said, and I heard the screech of duct tape being pulled.

They wrapped my ankles and twisted my arms back to wrap my wrists. Someone looped a mass of tape across my face to cover my mouth, pulling it tight along the back of my skull.

I looked around and saw Jane standing in the open doorway, surveying the bodies on the floor. She grabbed Prudence under the armpits and dragged her corpse away from the door. It seemed an act of kindness, out of place in this abattoir.

Others entered behind Jane, and I recognized the skeletal woman who had been hunted by the soldier I had killed.

"In here!" Jane called.

Maxwell and another man hauled me upright and dragged me into the warehouse. They pushed me onto the big table.

"Restrain him," Jane said.

One coiled a rope around my neck and tied it to the table so I couldn't lift my head. They slid a rope across my waist and my legs so I couldn't roll or thrash.

Jane picked through the tools on the work bench, and I got an inkling of what she had in mind. She chose a hack saw with a heavy steel blade. She leaned over, looked me in the eyes, and it was like gazing into my own reflection.

"Let's start with his legs," Jane said.

**

EPILOGUE:
I DIED YESTERDAY

You come here now, and listen to my story. Every week, new people gather in this theatre of pain to stare at me and hear my words. I smell you out there in the darkened seats, new scents, and recognize how I have become a sideshow freak used to educate your children about the dangers of the undead.

I am a traitor to my kind, but what of it? I survive, and that is the only law.

All that remains of me is this hunk of meat, this limbless torso and face. I do not rot away, though I desiccate if I am not fed. I never tire. I never sleep, though sometimes my awareness fades and the mindless period returns, when all I can do is snap my toothless jaws and moan.

They knocked out my teeth so I cannot bite you. They gouged out my eyes, because they don't want me to see you as you sit and listen; they fear that I might attack you if I could see you, if I could somehow crawl to you from off of this podium and out of these harnesses I wear. They keep me here in darkness and hunger, and I am not afraid to tell you that I would bite off your faces if I could.

Jane is long dead now. Maxwell is dead, and Moses, and Willy, and Nancy, and all the others. Years and years have passed while I have been trapped here. Generations of you cattle have reproduced unchecked, as I am forced to tell my story over and over again.

Humans have such short spans upon this earth. They live, and fuck, and die, struggling to survive all the days in between, and finally failing. It is what they do.

And I speak. Never ending. Time means nothing to me. I died yesterday, or a hundred years ago. I survive. That's what I do.

Sometimes, a person will come close to me and pour blood into my open mouth. Usually animal blood, but sometimes, and from what source I don't know, they will feed me human blood. You think I can't taste the difference? And for a little while, the hunger fades and my mind comes alive with memories of the weeks when I was free and ruled my world. I can feel my muscles growing strong again, feel the blood seeping from the wounds that will never heal.

I was not the first of my kind to awaken to awareness. I know that now because the humans have told me stories about them. And clearly, I was not the last. More and more of the things you call "zombies" began to awaken, and more of us were discovered by the humans. It was a new beginning to the zombie-human war, the battle for possession of the planet, the contest between the alpha predators.

They have told me stories of zombie enclaves that kept humans in breeding kennels, and — oh, how I wish I could have seen such a wonderful thing! My own plans were too small, I realize now. Too selfish. Maybe, if I had remained free a little longer, or if that damned woman had not been so fucking smart and capable.

No longer am I as distanced from my emotions as I was in the time just after I awoke. I have no problem saying what I feel. And I feel so many things, so very vibrantly.

Let me finish with this:

I hate you with all that I am. All that is left to me.

Given the slightest opportunity, I would hurt you in ways you could not even begin to imagine. I would eat you slowly, piece by piece. I would spread my affliction anew. I would build armies to take your cities, and we would go on forever, eating your children and grandchildren, ad infinitum, amen.

I hold out hope that, someday, the others of my kind will find this enclave and take you all to the meat house, and that I am there to hear your cries in the darkness and taste, once again, your mortal flesh.

ABOUT THE AUTHOR

Tony Simmons is the author of three previous novels: *Welcome to the Dawning of a New Century*, *The Book of Gabriel*, and *Dragon Rising*; a collection of short stories and miscellany, *The Best of Days*; and a collection of his award-winning newspaper columns, *Dazed and Raving in the Undercurrents*. He edited the two-volume *City Limits* anthology for the Panama City Centennial; produced *33 Days*, a collection of short fiction inspired by songs by The Offer; and has had numerous short stories published in anthologies. He lives in Panama City Beach, Florida, and works as a Digital Platform Manager, writer and editor with The News Herald and PanamaCity.com.

Learn more at his website, TonySimmons.info
Follow him on Twitter @midnightonmars
Like him on Facebook.com/WriterTonySimmons

Made in the USA
Charleston, SC
05 March 2015